The Search for Soren's Secrets

Mark A. Wullert

The following novel is entirely a work of fiction. Any resemblance to actual persons, living or dead is entirely coincidental.

First published in 2014 by QA Productions.

Cover art by Lynette Charters Serembe

THANK YOU

It takes a tremendous amount of time and effort from so many to bring a story from start to finish. The Search for Soren's Secrets could not have completed that journey without the patience, faith and support of so many.

To designer and artist Lynette Charters Serembe for making the cover art and the promotional images for the web site look so good, thank you.

To Lisa Mottola Hudon, who is a terrific editor and guiding force in bringing these stories from concept to the printed page.

To Hailey Jacobsen for proofreading this story in its early stages and inspiring me in all that you do.

To all of the librarians and media specialists at public libraries and in schools, thank you for the work you do to inspire a love of reading and for welcoming Luke and the rest of The Stolen Adventure gang into your libraries.

As always, my family is the key to every good thing that has ever happened in my life. So Lisa, Luke, Mark and Jake, thank you for all that you are and everything that you do.

And to Trey Kraw and everyone at QA Productions for your faith in me and your belief in The Stolen Adventure.

You Too Can Join the Adventure

Become a Member of
The Stolen Adventure Fan Club

www.stolenadventure.com

OR VISIT

www.facebook.com/TheStolenAdventure

CONTENTS

THE SEARCH FOR SOREN'S SECRETS

Prologue

"We want you to take us to Soren Jacobsen's chambers," Dad said. Despite the confidence in his strong, steady voice, he still had doubt. It was just beneath the surface, but it was there. He tried hard not to show it. A small film of perspiration formed on his face, giving him a shimmery shine like a fish at the early morning market. He pushed his glasses up the bridge of his nose, wiped the sweat from his brow and added, "We want to learn as much as we can."

Aunt Janine sat in the mission chair by the fireplace, her expression stern, her cold green eyes steely. She pondered the situation, thinking of ways this could be turned to her advantage.

It was hard to believe this was the same woman who, over the past year, left the Stolin family trapped in an underground chamber in Argentina, and then in Denmark, and then again in France; even harder to believe that circumstances had changed and she was now a welcome guest in their living room.

She studied Dad. He was different now than when they first met fourteen years ago, different now than he was one year ago, before this whole adventure came to a boil. Silently, she regretted his newfound confidence, and wondered how she could take it away. Her response, when it came, was cold and calculated. "And what makes you think I'm going to help you?" she asked.

1

"Because of what we know," Dad responded. He shifted uncomfortably before adding, "and what you don't want anyone else knowing."

As much as Aunt Janine tried not to react, she couldn't stop her lips from revealing a small grimace. "I'm going to help you," she said, "but not because you think you can blackmail me. There's a much bigger picture here and, as much as I hate to admit it, you and your boys are right in the middle of it."

Mom, who had been silent until now, gasped. She could not remain stoic, not when the safety of her boys was at stake. "Bigger picture?" she interjected. "What is the bigger picture? What exactly are we talking about? This is why we need to learn more."

A stunning woman stepped from the shadows and towards Aunt Janine. "That's why we need to take them," Abigail pleaded with her older sister, "to help them understand." She was beautiful. Not in a way portrayed by modern media, with in-your-face flash and gratuitousness. No, she was different. She was… elegant… and timeless, with a natural charm that brought a sense of peace to even the most dire of circumstances. When she spoke, everything else stopped.

Unlike the rest of the world, Janine was unfazed by Abigail's charms. She ignored her sister, turned to Dad and said, "You're talking about being away for a long time… a month, maybe two."

Dad, distracted by Abigail's beauty, had to collect himself, to return his focus to the problem at hand. He shifted his body towards Janine and said, "I'm hoping we can take care of what we need to do within a month. We need to be back for the boys."

"The boys," Mom added, "what will we do with the boys?"

Janine smiled. This was going perfectly. "You should bring the boys," she said, "it will be good for them to experience this and to learn as much as they can."

"Absolutely not," Mom replied. "We want to know more, but we're not putting the boys in the middle of this."

"Suit yourself," Janine replied; condescension dripped from every word. "You can only keep them under your wing for so long; at some point you need to cut the cord."

Mom shot back, "Is that your advice… from all of your *parenting* experience? You may know how to run a company, but you don't know anything about raising kids."

"Either way," Janine responded nonchalantly. She stood up and moved towards the door. "We'll be here to pick you up on the 24th." And with that, she walked out the front door. Abigail followed close on her heels. There was a long black limo idling in the driveway, waiting to take them away.

Before they got to the car, but out of earshot of Mom and Dad, Janine said, "That was perfect, they're doing exactly what we want and they think it's their idea."

* * *

Mom and Dad watched through the front window as Janine and Abigail got in the car and rode off. "Do you think we can trust them?" Mom asked.

3

"No," Dad replied matter of factly. "I'm sure we can't…that's why I've arranged for the information we have on her to be delivered automatically if we don't log in."

"Do you think it's enough? It didn't stop her from attacking us in France."

"In France I wasn't prepared," Dad said. "We had no idea she was going to be there. This time we know what to expect and everything will be pre-arranged."

"If you say so," Mom replied. Her facial muscles contorted awkwardly; the stress of the situation built up inside of her. She was unable to hide her concern. "So what are we going to do with the boys?

1. Getting Started

Luke and Tommy sat on their bedroom floor, enjoying the warmth of the Saturday morning sun. It was early June and it had been over a month since their latest adventure, going to a secret chamber in France with the Manillo family. It was hard to believe that Aunt Janine had Durendal, Sir Roland's sword; even harder to believe that Joyeuse, the magical sword that once belonged to King Charlemagne, had been in a museum just thirty miles from their home.

Their lives had returned to a level of normal, as much as it could for a bunch of kids who had risked life and death in search of a trio of powerful swords that could change the course of history.

Luke stood up and looked at himself in the mirror. He ran his fingers through his unkempt, sandy blonde hair and pushed his glasses up his nose. "Do you know what Mrs. Johansen said to me?" he said, as much to himself as to his brother and cousin in the room. "She said, 'If Curtana is back it's because the homeland needs protection. The kind of protection only the most powerful weapon in the world can provide.'"

"Protection from what?" Tommy asked, swishing his surfer blond hair out of his icy blue eyes with a flip of his head, not bothering to take his attention off of the super hero comic book that lay before him.

"Soren Jacobsen was a great inventor," Luke answered. "He not only created the magical pieces that Uncle Al sent us, but he also predicted that hundreds of years later we would bring those pieces together, put them in his magical clock and open Holger Danske's tomb. He chose us for a reason. He chose that I should have Curtana. But why? And what are we supposed to do next?"

Tommy looked at his brother quizzically. "Am I supposed to know the answer to that?"

Luke broke eye contact with his reflection in the mirror and looked down. There, on the top of the dresser, was a copy of Hans Jacobsen's journal. This journal, written by the grandson of the master inventor, was the only remaining link to the man and his secrets. A thought came to Luke's mind. "I know what we're gonna do this summer," he said with a gleam in his eye. "It's time to take the bull by the horns."

"What does that mean?" Tommy asked

"I think it means we're going to Spain?" Katie, Luke and Tommy's quick-witted and fast talking cousin, said. She was spread out on Tommy's bed, involved in her own bit of reading, a fashion and style magazine.

"No... it's a figure of speech," Luke said. "For the past year we've been going on these wild adventures without even knowing where we're going or what we're after. I think it's time we start to control our own direction."

"And how are we going to do that?" Tommy asked, still lacking the excitement that Luke was trying to generate. "Are there more swords?"

"I don't know."

"Did Hans write another journal?" Katie asked, still paging through her magazine.

"I don't know that either."

6

"So what do you know?" Katie inquired.

"Not much apparently," Tommy quipped.

"That's not true," Luke defended, "I know where we've been."

"Yeah, so."

"And you can't really know where you're going until you fully understand where you've been."

"You're confusing us; just get to the point."

"This," Luke answered, dropping Hans' journal on the bed next to his cousin.

"You mean?" Katie asked, starting to gain interest.

"Yep," Luke replied, his smile spread from ear to ear.

"I don't get it," Tommy cut in, "someone fill me in."

Katie picked up the journal and started paging through the contents. "Uncle Al always said it's a treasure map."

"That's crazy," Tommy replied, finally understanding what Luke was trying to say. "Those places are all over the world, and besides, Uncle Al and Aunt Janine have already been there; they took the clock and the magical pieces."

"But think of everything they didn't take," Luke responded. "Think of what they may have missed, or things they know that they never told us. Remember all the writings on the walls in the chamber in Argentina or the mural on the ceiling in Kronborg? They were all messages from Soren Jacobsen. Who knows what we could learn, they might even tell us what we're supposed to do next."

"You have to admit," Katie said, "it would make for a pretty exciting summer. We'd be archaeologists. Even if we didn't find anything new, we'd still get to see all of the chambers that Soren Jacobsen built."

7

Tommy balked, "Okay, maybe it would be cool to get to see all those places but do you realize where we're talking about? Greece, Poland, Russia, how exactly do you think we're going to get there? After what happened in France and at the museum, we'll be lucky if Mom and Dad let us go out in the backyard."

"Actually, they're planning to send us away for the summer, to Camp Forsyth."

"To Camp Forsyth?" Tommy replied. "How do you know that?"

"I overheard them talking the other night."

"And you didn't tell me?"

Luke shrugged his shoulders indifferently.

"But we didn't do anything wrong," Tommy protested. "It was Aunt Janine who came after us. What did we do to deserve that?"

"They want us safe and they think we'll be safe at Camp Forsyth."

"That's not fair."

"I have a plan," Luke stated. He knelt down between his brother and cousin. "Are you in?" He put his hand out in front of them.

"I'm in," Katie replied, placing her hand on top of Luke's.

"I'm not going to Camp Forsyth," Tommy replied defiantly. He placed his hand on top of Katie's. "So what's the plan?"

2. Working the Plan

For most kids, the last day of school is a time for celebration. Another year completed, and a summer filled with lazy days by the pool and lots of free time. When you're headed to a military style summer camp, it's a moment of dread, a summer with so much work and discipline that you can't wait for September and the return to school.

Luke met Tommy on the bus for the ride home. They huddled close together, going over their plan one more time. Each action had to be performed with the utmost care and attention to detail, or else the scheme wouldn't work. They both knew their part, but they couldn't help but to be nervous; so much was riding on what would happen over the next couple of hours.

When the school bus pulled up in front of their house, Mom, Dad and their 3 year old brother, Billy, were waiting in the driveway. Mom had tears in her eyes. She agreed that it was best for the boys to spend the summer safe and sound at a military camp, but that didn't mean she liked the idea. Billy was beside himself with glee; he reveled in being the only child for the summer, getting all of Mom and Dad's attention without being picked on by his older brothers. Dad was busy loading up the van, making sure that everything was all set for the trip.

"Give me a hug," Mom said to her boys as they made their way down the driveway. She fought the urge to cry.

"Go in and use the bathroom," Dad instructed. "We have a long drive ahead of us and I don't want to be making unnecessary stops."

Luke broke away from his mother and headed into the house, Tommy was right behind him. As soon as they were inside, and out of Mom and Dad's sight, Tommy snuck into Dad's office while Luke went to their room.

Upstairs, Luke quickly crawled under the bed, removed part of the baseboard in the corner and opened a hidden safe. He removed two small pre-packed satchels, one for Tommy and one for himself. He rushed to close everything and get back downstairs before anyone realized what he was doing. Luckily, Mom, Dad and Billy were still outside.

Tommy came out of Dad's office as Luke came down the steps. He took one of the satchels from Luke's outstretched hand.

"Did you get it?" Luke asked.

Tommy patted his stomach to let Luke know that he was successful in his mission, and that the prize was tucked neatly beneath his belt. "Why do you think Dad had it in his office?" Tommy asked.

"Who knows," Luke replied, "he's always studying something."

They pounded fists, ready for the next phase of their mission. They headed for the front door just as Mom walked in. "Are you boys okay? What's taking so long?"

"Just saying goodbye to all of our stuff," Tommy responded sullenly, "before you ship us off."

"It's not like that," Mom balked. "It's just that you'll be safer there."

Tommy didn't like the answer any more now than he did the first hundred times he heard it. He avoided Mom's eyes, storming past her and out the door.

The remaining items were packed in the van, and they were on the road, headed north to Camp Forsyth. The conversation was sparse; Mom struggled to say anything, still unsure of whether she could handle being away from her boys for an entire summer. Dad stayed intent on the road, cursing the Friday afternoon traffic.

Camp Forsyth was a two-hour ride up the Northeast extension of the Pennsylvania Turnpike, nestled discreetly in the Pocono Mountains. It was known for its military style discipline. Many boys were assigned to Camp Forsyth by court order, as an alternative to juvenile detention. It had been said that once a boy spent a summer at Camp Forsyth, he would never step out of line again. Luke and Tommy still couldn't believe they were being sent there. The only thing they had done was to be victimized by an evil woman in her plot to rule the world.

"You know boys," Dad explained in his usual scientific manner, "Camp Forsyth may have a reputation for discipline, but it can really be a lot of fun. Did you know that your Uncle Al and I both spent a summer there?"

"You did?"

"Yep," Dad replied. "It was right after your Uncle Al stole our neighbor's '49 Studebaker and took it for a joyride. He ended up crashing it into a tree. Boy was my father mad."

"So you mean you guys deserved it?" Tommy said.

"Well, maybe your Uncle Al did..." Dad thought back to those days. "But I really had a great time. That summer I learned a lot about myself. After that, I never fooled around again. It was just hard work from there on out."

Mom gasped. She was still wrestling with the idea of sending the boys to this camp, and couldn't bear the thought of them losing the innocence of youth, but she also had a vision of what the future had in store for them, and she wanted them as prepared as possible.

The van cruised North, up the PA Turnpike and then up Interstate 81. Dad veered off the highway on a nondescript dirt road. No signs, no markers, just a beaten path that led into the thick brush of the mountains. A couple of miles in, the road ended at a rundown shack.

3. On Arrival

The van skidded to a stop. Dad pressed a button and the side door opened. "Here we are," he said.

"Here?" Luke asked. "There's nothing here."

Before they could get out, a young man in a pressed khaki uniform stepped out from the shack. He wore a red sash across his chest, a matching red beret on his head, and a large knife strapped to his belt. What they could see of his hair was cropped close to his scalp. His voice rang with a cacophonous boom, "Welcome to Camp Forsyth!"

He may have said the words "welcome to," but his tone was not welcoming in the least. In fact, the discipline and authority that he emitted did not have the slightest trace of anything positive.

Tommy got out of the van and looked around. "Where's the camp?" he asked.

"You travel to the camp on foot," the young man responded. "Two miles due north."

Luke and Tommy looked first to Mom, who turned away to hide her tears, and then to Dad, who had a gleam in his eye.

"Your compasses are in your packs," Dad responded. "Remember what he said, 'due north.'"

Dad pulled their packs from the back of the van and helped them load them onto their backs. "By the end of this summer you'll be disciplined young men, ready for anything."

13

Billy scampered around their feet while Luke and Tommy struggled with the idea of marching two miles into the wooded forest just to get to Camp Forsyth. Tommy tried to catch Luke's eye; he was beginning to question whether or not their plan would work.

Dad secured the last strap on Luke then turned to his youngest son. "C'mon Billy, you're next."

"Billy?!? Billy can't come here," Tommy balked.

In an instant, the look on Billy's face turned from total glee to absolute horror.

"You can't make Billy go here; this is a military camp," Luke objected.

"Billy needs this just as much as you do," Dad said. "Trust me, by the time you boys finish the summer, you'll be prepared for anything."

Luke's mind began to race. He still held out hope that his plan to escape Camp Forsyth would work, even with the long trek through the forest, but not with Billy; this changed everything. They couldn't make the trip with him and they certainly couldn't leave him there alone.

"Dad," Luke protested, "we understand that we have to go, but Billy? You can't make Billy go through this."

Dad ignored his oldest son. He attached the pack to Billy's back and adjusted all of the straps, securing it tightly to his small frame. Billy began sobbing, still unsure that this was really happening.

"Mom," Luke pleaded, "you can't send Billy; he's only three."

Mom knew what she and Dad had agreed to, and as difficult as it was, she knew what needed to be done. With tears in her eyes and a pained expression on her face, she rolled up her window and turned away.

Dad tightened the last strap on Billy's pack then turned to Luke and Tommy. "Okay boys, you heard what the man said, Camp is two miles due north. You better get started; you'll want to make it there before nightfall." He extended a hand, offering to shake Luke and Tommy's hands before they headed off for an entire summer of military discipline.

The boys were bewildered. They started on the path, stunned and confused, giving several looks over their shoulders to confirm that this was really happening.

The young man in uniform repeated, "Two miles due north." In a lower voice, meant just for them, he added, "Just stick to the path and you'll be okay."

With one final look back, the boys offered a meek wave and headed on their way.

Mom jumped from the van and ran toward the boys. "Wait!"

"That's it," Luke said to himself; a smile formed on his lips, "this was all just a test, they weren't really going to make us go to Camp Forsyth. They just wanted to scare us."

The young man in uniform stepped in front of Mom. With raised hands he boomed, "No parents beyond this point."

"At least let me say goodbye," she called.

"Goodbye?" Luke thought. "Can this really be happening?"

Billy ran back and leapt into his mother's arms. "Please, I want to go with you," he cried.

"You have to, honey," Mom said through sobs and tears. "It's for the best."

Luke and Tommy returned, gave Mom a final hug and pulled a crying Billy away. They headed down the path as Dad ushered Mom back to the van.

Once they were out of sight of the shack, Tommy asked, "Luke is this really happening?"

Luke looked over his shoulder to make sure they were out of earshot before answering, "We may have Billy with us, but that's not changing anything. We have a plan and were sticking to it." He looked down at the compass and added, "Katie's waiting for us; we need to get moving."

4. Making a Break

"Are you sure we're doing the right thing?" Mom asked.

Dad turned the van off of the dirt road and back onto the highway. "We've been over this," he responded. "They'll be safe there, much safer than if they were with us... and they'll learn some valuable lessons, things that will help them survive."

"I guess so," Mom agreed. "It just feels like we left them in the middle of nowhere."

Dad pulled the van off to the side of the road. "Do you think we should go back and get them? We can take them with us."

Mom thought about it for a moment before answering, "No, I don't think that would be safe."

"Then we're decided?" Dad asked.

"Yes."

He merged back onto the highway. "Then let's not talk about it anymore; we have enough to worry about."

* * *

Luke, Tommy, and Billy hiked the trail to Camp Forsyth. About a mile in, they broke away from the main path and headed east into the densest part of the woods. There was no trail in this direction, only thick brush and rocky terrain. Luke checked his compass to make sure they were heading in the right direction. "According to my calculations, we should reach Route 1015 in less than a mile."

"Aren't they going to start searching for us when we don't show up?" Tommy asked, shielding himself from the branches that whipped back from Luke as he led the way.

"I took care of that," Luke explained. "Right about now Katie is sending an email to the director explaining that Mom and Dad had a change of plans and would not be sending us to camp for the summer."

"Do you think they're really going to believe an email?"

"No, I don't. But I logged into the registration account from Dad's computer and changed all of the contact information. So when they call to verify, they're going to call Katie's cell phone. She knows what to do when they call."

"If you say so," Tommy replied, still unsure. The combination of the setting sun and the thick canopy of leaves from the trees made the forest very dark and rather scary. "So what are we going to do when we get to Route 1015 in the middle of the night?"

"We just have to make it to the intersection of 1015 and Hickory Ridge by 9 o'clock," Luke said. "We have plenty of time." Luke looked down at his watch. "It's only 7:30 now."

No sooner had the words left his mouth than he wished he could take them back. They pushed through a particularly thick area of brush to come face to face with a twelve-foot high wall of stone. A man-made barrier, no doubt put in place by the founders of Camp Forsyth to keep people out, or… to keep prisoners in. Either way, it went on in either direction as far as the eye could see and posed a distinct problem for Luke's plan.

"How are we getting over that?" Tommy asked.

"I'm thinking," Luke replied. He was thinking, but no answers were coming. The ridges of the wall were too thin for any footholds, and the trees nearest to the wall were only saplings--too small to provide any help.

Tommy tried to scale the wall. He managed to get half way up, wedging himself between a couple small trees and the wall, to shimmy several feet. But he could go no further. There was nothing to grab as he reached higher on the wall.

Luke sized up the situation. He walked along the wall and around the surrounding area. He bent a few trees back, contemplating using the small saplings as a catapult, but quickly abandoned the idea. A little further away he found what he was looking for. "Tommy come here, I have an idea."

Tommy rushed over. Luke stood next to a fallen tree. "If we can pick up this tree, we can prop it against the wall and use it to climb over."

It sounded like a good idea, certainly better than any other option. Together they set to work trying to lift the large trunk. The sheer size of the tree, combined with the lack of any tools, made the job impossible. After thirty minutes of dirty, sweaty work, they gave up.

"We can't let this stupid wall stop us," Luke shouted, kicking the tree in frustration.

A sound in the distance caught their attention. It sent chills up their spines. Luke knew exactly what the sound was, but hesitated to tell Tommy. One look at his brother let him know that he already knew.

Tommy began to hyperventilate. "Luke, do you hear that?"

"Hear what?" Luke said, but he knew all too well what Tommy was referring to.

"That sound, it... it... it sounds like... dogs." His breathing became faster and in between huffs he asked, "Where's Billy?"

Luke furtively scanned the area. Panic began to set in. "Oh no." It was getting late and what little daylight they had was fading away. The sound, that only moments ago had been off in the distance, grew louder. There was no mistaking it now. It was barking and not just one, but several canines. Were they wild dogs? Were they guard dogs from the camp? What would they do when they got there? They couldn't be sure, but they needed to find Billy, and soon. Luke pulled a flashlight from his pack and shined it all around. "Billy," he called.

No response came.

Tommy grabbed a flashlight from his pack and moved in the opposite direction, trying to control his breathing. "Billy, where are you?" Panic seeped through every vein. Was this trip really a good idea? They couldn't even get out of the woods, how were they going to get half way around the world? Then, he heard a reassuring sound over the wind that whistled through the trees and the dogs that continued to get closer with every passing moment.

It was Billy, giggling.

"Where are you Billy?" Tommy screamed, scanning the area with his flashlight.

Luke heard it too and came running. "Billy!" he called, "I heard you. Come out now!"

Both flashlights searched the area. At the base of the wall they found what they were looking for, Billy covered in dirt, smiling from ear to ear.

Tommy ran over and grabbed his little brother. He pulled him into a hug. "Don't ever do that again."

"Tommy…" Luke interrupted.

By now the dogs were gaining fast. Even in the receding light they could see them barreling through the brush.

Tommy yelled, "W…w...w…we n…n…need t…t…to g…g…get outta here!"

Luke pointed to the ground. "Billy found the answer. He dug a hole under the wall. How do you think he did that?"

"Who cares," Tommy shouted. The dogs were now through the thickest of the bushes, and bounding toward them. There were three dogs, Rotweilers, and they looked angry-- teeth bared and slobber drooling from their mouths.

Billy slid through hole. Luke followed right behind. Tommy slid his feet through and then shimmied his body, but when he got to his shoulders, he was too big to fit. "Luke help!!!" The dogs were upon him.

5. Doggie Dinner

Tommy flailed with his arms, trying to keep the dogs at bay. There were three of them, and they were vicious. He pushed the first one, but another bit at his arm, tearing his shirt and narrowly missing his flesh. Another circled and snapped at his other arm, snagging his shirtsleeve and tearing him like a rag doll. He was trapped, pulled in opposite directions by two growling canines. The first dog recovered from the initial push and stepped forward. He bared his teeth and lunged at Tommy's face.

Despite the two powerful dogs pulling him by the sleeves, Tommy managed to twist his body and duck his head. The motion was just enough to get under the dog's jaw and bring the crown of his head into the dog's neck. The snarling canine retreated momentarily, but then attacked again, launching himself, and snapping his jaw at Tommy's nose.

There was nothing Tommy could do. He envisioned the gouging he was about to take from the sharp incisors. He'd lost all hope when his feet were pulled out from under him, yanked through the hole beneath the wall, leaving his sleeves in tattered shreds in the mouths of the unsuspecting dogs.

Tommy scampered to his feet and backed away in fright. The dogs lunged their bodies at the hole, struggling to get through. They could not maneuver the angle, but kept coming, nosing their way through the opening, barking and snarling until Luke pushed a large stone into the gap, sealing the hole and leaving the frustrated dogs on the other side.

Tommy breathed a huge sigh of relief, looking at what was left of his tattered shirt. He wrapped his arms around Luke and gave him a giant hug. Then he turned to his little brother and picked him up. "You're awesome," he said, squeezing him tight. "How did you do that?"

Billy held up a small silver tool that looked like a mini flashlight, and laughed out loud.

"You little bugger," Tommy said, stretching for the object. It was the tool that Billy had found a couple of months ago, on their trip to France with the Manillo family, to study Sir Roland's hidden chamber.

"Mine!" Billy said, pulling it close to his chest.

"I know," Tommy laughed. "It's yours."

The rest of the hike through the woods was difficult, but passable. They made it to Route 1015, which turned out to be an unlit country road. Another mile and a half of walking brought them to a single street lamp and the intersection of Route 1015 and Hickory Ridge Road.

"So we're here," Tommy said. He dropped his pack to the ground and took a new shirt from his backpack. "What now?" he asked.

"It's 8:45," Luke replied. "Now we wait."

* * *

The yellow cab was late; it pulled up at ten minutes past nine, stopping directly beneath the streetlight at the intersection of Route 1015 and Hickory Ridge Road. The driver honked his horn and looked around, skeptical that there

23

really was someone there for his services, ready to take off at the first sign of anything unusual.

Luke, Tommy and Billy emerged from the shadows and approached the idling car. "You're late," Luke said to the driver.

He was an older man with dark skin, a scraggly beard and moustache, and a turban on his head. "I am thinking this is some kind of prank," he responded. His accent was heavy, from somewhere in India, Luke thought. "You're making me to drive out to the middle of nowhere," the man added. He eyed the three young boys suspiciously. "Where are your parents?"

Luke, Tommy and Billy were a sight to be seen. They were all sweaty and covered in dirt. "They're meeting us at the airport," Luke responded firmly. "They're going to be worried sick if we're late."

"You should not be out so late," the driver scolded. "Where is it you are to be coming from?"

"We were on a camping trip," Luke replied as they loaded their gear into the back seat.

"Why do I now pick you up under streetlamp in the middle of nowhere?" the driver continued. "Something is not right."

Luke leaned forward and handed the driver a crisp hundred.

The man snatched it from his hand, placed it on the dash and used a marker to check that it was real. Once he was convinced of its authenticity, his attitude changed. "Welcome aboard," he said with a smile. "What airport are we going?"

"Scranton International," Luke said. "Continental Airlines."

The taxi lurched into *Drive* and they were on their way. There was no conversation. In the back seat, Luke silently contemplated his plan, Tommy nursed the scrapes on his legs and arms, and Billy played with his magical toy. Up front, the driver stayed intent on the road.

About thirty minutes later, they pulled up to the curb for Continental departures. Tommy and Billy jumped out of the backseat, dragging their packs behind them. Luke leaned toward the driver. "I'll take my change now."

"The fare is $80," the man exclaimed.

"So that means I get $20 change," Luke said.

"It is customary to offer a gratuity for excellent service," the driver responded.

"All you did was drive," Luke retorted.

"Perhaps we should let your parents decide." He looked over Luke's shoulder, scanning the area. "Where are your parents?"

Luke started to panic, he didn't want to give up the twenty dollars, but he also couldn't wait for parents that were never going to show up. He wasn't sure what to do. The driver stared him down, a devilish smile across his face. Luke's body began to shake. A voice startled them both. "There you are... Mom and Dad are at the counter and they need your passport." Katie leaned her head inside the back of the cab. "What's the hold up?" Luke sighed with relief. It was good to see Katie.

"He won't give me my change," he said, the anxiety slowly leaving his body.

25

Katie looked the driver directly in the eyes. "Do we need to call security?" She pointed towards a man in uniform just ten feet away.

The driver took one look at the security guard and knew he didn't want any trouble. He stuttered, "N-n-n-no, but a gratuity would be appreciated."

"Give us the change and we'll make sure you are properly compensated," Katie replied. She spoke with authority. Luke was amazed at her confidence. Sheepishly, the man turned over two fives and a ten.

Katie returned the ten-dollar bill. "Thank you," she said triumphantly. Together she and Luke backed out of the cab. The driver raced away.

"Ten dollars?" Luke said as they watched the taxi zoom off. "We have to be careful how much we spend."

"Would it be better if we got the police involved?" Katie questioned.

"No," Luke replied, "but we have an unexpected traveler... Billy's with us."

"Make that two unexpected travelers, Lynn's with us too."

6. Breaking from the Plan

Under normal circumstances Billy and Lynn were a handful, they could cause trouble just about anywhere. But here, at the airport, ready to board an international flight, they were a major problem. The original plan didn't include traveling with two three year olds. It was going to be a difficult mission already, but add in two incorrigible toddlers, and now it was nearly impossible.

"How are we going to travel around the world with them?" Luke asked.

"They can be good when they want to be," Tommy replied in defense of his younger brother and cousin.

"We don't have tickets for them," Luke explained, "and we don't have their passports."

Katie was down on her knees, talking in earnest with her sister. When she stood up, she had a glow about her, a familiar glow that came about whenever she had an idea. "Let's go to the bathroom," she said. "I have an idea."

Luke and Tommy exchanged a confused glance, but followed her all the same. They paused when they got to the restroom door. "We can't go in there; that's the ladies room."

"We need someplace private to talk and this is the best we're going to get." Katie pushed the boys through the doorway and into the women's bathroom. Thankfully, there was no one else there.

Tommy looked about in awed wonder. "This isn't much different from the men's room, but where are the urinals?"

27

Katie gave him a playful slap to the back of the head. "We don't use urinals, you dip."

"Oh yeah, right. But why do you have a couch in here? Do you take naps?"

Katie rolled her eyes then pinched his ear and dragged him toward the handicap stall. The others followed. It was large enough for all of them. Billy and Lynn immediately started playing with the toilet paper, sending the roll spiraling all over the floor.

"So here's what we do…" Katie explained.

* * *

Katie was the first one out of the ladies' room. She checked that the coast was clear and then signaled for Luke and Tommy to come out. They each dragged an overstuffed backpack. A few giggles and laughs came out of the packs.

"Shhh, you have to be quiet in there," Tommy scolded.

"This is never going to work," Luke mumbled under his breath.

Out of the side of her mouth, Katie whispered, "Just be quiet and follow the plan."

They approached the ticketing counter where an attendant greeted them. Her disposition was less than cheerful. "Tickets please," the woman barked robotically.

Katie placed her ticket on the counter.

"Are you checking any bags?"

Katie looked at Tommy who, with a struggle, hoisted one of the bags up onto the scale. From inside the bag, Billy let out a low moan and a giggle when the bag bounced.

"ID please," the woman said.

"ID?" Katie asked.

"You have to have ID in order to fly, dear."

"Oh…my passport." Katie rifled through her carry-on bag, withdrew her passport, and handed it to the woman.

The woman examined the photo and looked Katie up and down. "You're kind of young to be traveling alone. Where are your parents?"

"We're meeting them in Paris," Katie lied.

"Uh, uh," the woman scolded. "No one under the age of thirteen travels alone without UM credentials."

"UM credentials?"

"Unaccompanied Minor!" the woman stated emphatically.

Katie balked, "Uh…uh… he's thirteen," she said with a point to Luke.

"Fine," the woman responded, "then he can fly, but what about you?"

Katie never got a chance to say another word.

"Uh, oh! We got trouble!" Tommy announced.

A deep booming voice gathered their attention, "You bet you do, son."

7. The Departure

Mom waited nervously by the window, staring out at the driveway. The setting sun disappeared below the horizon as the sky slowly changed from blue to black. "Are we really going to do this?" she said, absentmindedly biting at her cuticles, being sure to keep her fingernails intact.

Her brother, Uncle Brian, placed a hand on her shoulder. "I'll be with you every step of the way. There's nothing to be worried about."

Aunt Eileen came out from the kitchen. She was dressed in waxed denim skinny jeans, a black cashmere sweater and a single strand of white pearls around her neck. She had her hair pulled back in a tight ponytail, and a cup of steaming Chai Latte in her hand. "No offense, but when your sister-in-law is involved, there's always something to be worried about. That woman is crazy."

Uncle Brian shot her a warning glance.

"What? It's true. When have we been involved with her when things didn't go bad?"

"I'm trying to calm her down," Uncle Brian snapped. "Besides, you know we're going on an expedition; what are you wearing?

"This is my casual attire," Aunt Eileen responded, spinning on her black, Dolce, high heeled boots.

"Brian's right," Dad said from the dining room table, not bothering to pick his head up from his computer. "We're going to be visiting cemeteries and underground vaults; you should really have better footwear."

"You said to wear boots and these are my boots," Aunt Eileen responded defensively.

Mom interrupted, "They're here. Are you sure we're ready for this?"

A large black limo pulled into the driveway. Aunt Janine, dressed in a black pinstripe suit, stepped out of the vehicle and sauntered up to the front door. The beautiful countenance of Abigail was right behind. Her glowing smile accented her picture perfect face, her blond hair floated in the breeze. Two men followed. The first was as large as a refrigerator, with a strong jaw and a buzz cut on his square head. A tattoo of a bloody sword adorned the overgrown muscles where his neck should have been. Next to him was a smallish man, or at least he looked small next to the mountain of a man. This man had a hollow face with narrow, pointy features, barely enough hair to cover the top of his head, but a bushy moustache that smothered his upper lip. No-Neck and the Walrus approached.

Mom opened the door to let them in. Uncle Brian immediately gathered all of their travel bags, ready for the trip. Mom, Dad, and Uncle Brian each had one bag. Aunt Eileen had narrowed all of her necessities down to three oversized suitcases. Dad ran about, taking care of a few last minute items while the group made small talk by the front door.

"I said to only pack the necessities," Aunt Janine scoffed. "We need to travel light."

Uncle Brian rolled his eyes as he and No-Neck gathered the bags and headed out the door. The whole group exited the house and headed to the waiting limo.

8. Not So Fast

Back at the airport, Luke turned to see who was talking to them, only to be greeted by the meanest, most snarling face he had ever seen. The buzz cut head and starched uniform made it clear that this could only be one person, Major Grill, the head of Camp Forsyth. Luke's first instinct was to run, to escape this situation and get away from the man who would most assuredly drag them back to Camp Forsyth for discipline and hard labor. But they weren't alone; Billy and Lynn were cooped up inside rolling luggage, ready to fly to Europe as baggage. It was not in his DNA to surrender, but what choice did he have.

It turned out this rational frame of thought was right, for the Major was not alone. Just a few paces in every direction were more uniforms, some filled by men looking down on them with disapproving glances, and others by seasoned cadets who looked even more disgruntled over the attempted escape.

"Did you really think you could get away with this?" the Major barked. "We were on your trail five minutes after you missed check-in!"

Luke couldn't help but doubt these words. Even with the dogs in the woods, they had made it pretty far, off the grounds of Camp Forsyth and to the airport. If it hadn't been for Billy and Lynn they would have already been through customs and getting ready to board their flight. What would the Major have done then? The real question was, how did they know to come to the airport? Just then Luke caught a glimpse of the cab driver that picked them up. The man offered a taunting laugh when he caught Luke's eye.

"I should have given a bigger tip," Luke said.

Major Grill grabbed Luke by the arm and ushered him towards the door. "That was one of your mistakes," he said, "your biggest was thinking you could get one over on me."

They passed through the rotating door and out to the curb where a Camp Forsyth van was waiting. "Sir," a cadet addressed the Major, "what about these two?" he asked, directing the Major's attention to Katie and Lynn.

Major Grill took one look at the two girls and sneered. "They're not our problem."

If she could have, Katie would have reached over and wiped the smug, sneering grin right off of the Major's face, but unfortunately her arm was being held by the cadet's hand.

"Let her find her own way home," the Major added, "she's someone else's problem."

"We're not going anywhere without them," Katie shouted.

"Correction... you're not going *with* them." The Major pushed Luke, Tommy and Billy into the awaiting van.

Another uniformed man approached the cadet and, in a soft voice said, "Get them a cab and send them home." The cadet did as he was told, guiding Katie away from the van and towards a row of waiting cabs. Lynn followed close behind, bewildered by the events unfolding before her. The first cabbie in line jumped out of his car and opened the back door of his taxi, "Where to?" he asked eagerly.

The cadet turned to Katie. "Hartsville," she replied with a wry smile, "just north of Philly."

The cabbie's eyes lit up at the words. He grabbed Katie's bag, threw it in the back of the cab and held the door for the girls to climb in. He turned to the cadet, "You pay?" he asked.

"I can't pay you," the young man balked.

The cabbie looked at the other men in uniform. One by one they shook their heads. Depressed, the cabbie turned back to the girls in the back seat where Katie was holding out her hand. "Do you take Visa?"

9. An Empty House

The trip from the airport was uneventful to say the least. The Major ordered one of the cadets to drive the boys. He had close cropped hair and wore a starched, khaki uniform with a hunter green sash and beret. The green color was a symbol of his status, but his scowl of discontent made it clear this assignment did not properly recognize his achievements.

No conversation was allowed. The cadet wouldn't turn on the radio and probably wouldn't have let Luke, Tommy or Billy breathe if he thought they were enjoying it. At the moment he was downright bitter, and there were no signs that this was going to change any time soon.

They were on the road for twenty minutes before he finally broke the silence. "No cadet has ever escaped from Camp Forsyth before," he growled, "a record we were very proud of, until you boys trashed it. This type of insubordination, this transgression, will not be tolerated."

The cadet went on, "Why would anyone even want to leave? Camp Forsyth is the greatest place on God's green earth."

At first Luke thought they would be returned and forced into hours upon hours of hard manual labor. But the van cruised right by the exit for the camp and continued down the highway. It was then that Luke realized there was something much worse in store for them.

The Major's last words still hung in the air, "Only the best and the brightest, the most committed, are permitted to

35

grace the hallowed grounds of Camp Forsyth." They were no longer welcome at Camp Forsyth, and would be returned home as the only boys ever to be booted from the camp.

"I thought it was mostly juvenile delinquents," Tommy questioned. "Why are we being sent home?"

"SILENCE!" the young man screamed. "It'll be a cold day in Hades before I want to hear what you scofflaws have to say." It was apparent that the cadet didn't have high regard for the opinion of children, especially a trio of boys who had the audacity to disrespect Camp Forsyth. He did see fit, however, to drive them all the way home, even though a cab, just three car lengths back, was transporting Katie and Lynn to virtually the same location.

The Major had ordered the cadet to take them home. He also wanted him to reveal exactly what they had done and why they were no longer welcome at a camp designed to discipline the worst of the worst. Luke thought about what Dad would say; he thought about what Mom would say. It wasn't going to be pretty. He could only imagine what punishment was in store for them. With each passing mile, the impending doom grew closer and closer. By the time they pulled into the driveway, Luke's anxiety had grown to a fever pitch. He wasn't sure if it was a good thing or a bad thing when the cadet knocked on the door and no one answered.

They sat in the driveway in silence. First the cadet called Mom's cell phone, and then Dad's, all with no luck. "What kind of parents are completely unreachable?" he balked. "I'm beginning to see where you boys get your discipline. It's hard to believe your father was a cadet at Camp Forsyth. Things must have been different back then."

Tommy, annoyed by the way the man was talking about Mom and Dad, was about to say something when Luke's foot caught him in the shin. He turned on Luke, but was stopped by a single finger that Luke raised to his lips. Luke had a plan.

"Excuse me Sir?" Luke said as respectfully as he could.

The young man snapped his head around and glared at Luke, hatred seething from his eyes. His face was crimson red and the veins on his temples were raised and throbbing.

Luke backed away, unsure if he should proceed with his plan. He gathered his courage and said, "I...I...I have a key, I could let us in. I know you have a long drive ahead of you. It's late."

"You think I'm going to let you off that easy? That I'm just going to drop you off without letting your parents know the trouble you've caused?"

"No," Luke answered resolutely. His confidence increased, a strange calm grew within him. "It's just that... it's after midnight and I don't think they're going to be home tonight. They didn't know we were coming and they probably went to visit friends."

"You're not getting off that easy," the young man retorted. His words were icy, but the venom in his voice was waning. He contemplated Luke's suggestion.

"No... but... you're going to have to make that two hour drive whether it's now... or two hours from now. Either way, it's not like you're going to see them tonight."

The cadet looked at him steely-eyed, but said nothing.

Luke continued, "Besides, you're still going to tell our parents and we're going to get in deep trouble. There's no way we can explain getting booted out of your camp."

It took a while, but eventually the man came around to Luke's way of thinking. Finally, he got out of the van, tossed their bags on the front lawn, and ordered them out of the vehicle. "You're not my problem anymore," he barked, and before they could reply, he raced out of the driveway and was on his way.

10. Reviewing the Tape

Luke helped Billy to bed. Once he had his little brother settled, Luke rushed downstairs to address the important question. Where were Mom and Dad? Of course they couldn't have been expecting their three sons to come home two months early from camp, but that didn't explain why they couldn't be reached on their cell phones. And it didn't explain why both of their cars were still in the driveway.

Maybe they really had gone to visit friends like Luke told the cadet. Maybe they took a trip and got a shuttle to the airport? All of that was possible, but why couldn't they be reached on their cell phones?

Luke found Tommy in the kitchen eating. "So where do you think Mom and Dad are?" he asked.

"I dunno," Tommy replied, stuffing the last bit of a ham sandwich into his mouth. "But I'm glad they had food in the fridge."

Luke headed towards Dad's office. "I'm going to check some things."

"What are you looking for?" Tommy asked, shuffling after Luke, still chomping on his sandwich.

"There has to be some clue as to where Mom and Dad are; I need to find the phone number for their bank so I can see where they last used their credit cards."

Tommy fiddled around with the things on Dad's desk while Luke found the phone number and dialed. After punching a bunch of numbers into the keypad and listening to the automated response, Luke hung up the phone. "They haven't used their credit cards in the past four days."

"So what do we do now?"

"I have an idea," Luke replied, "we can track their phones. They have the protection app, even if their phones aren't on, we can still see where they are."

Luke logged onto Dad's computer and started pecking away at the keyboard. "I just activated the GPS locator… uh oh!"

"What, what is it?" Tommy asked.

"They're here," Luke responded.

"That's great," Tommy said. He looked out the window. "Did they just pull up in the driveway?"

"No. Their phones… their phones are here… in the house. Look." Luke pointed to the center of the map on the screen. Two blinking lights hovered over their address in Hartsville, Pennsylvania.

Luke and Tommy scrambled around the house, looking for their parents. They looked in every room, they looked in the basement, they even looked in the attic, but they were nowhere to be found.

"Where could they be?" Tommy asked.

"I know… the desk in the dining room," Luke replied.

"They're in the desk?" Tommy said jokingly.

"Not them," Luke laughed, "their phones." Luke opened the slant front desk and pointed at the two phones still connected to the chargers. "Here they are."

"But Mom and Dad never go out without their phones," Tommy replied.

"I know."

"Brnnnng!" The ringing of the house phone startled them. Luke raced into the kitchen and grabbed the receiver. "Mom? Dad?"

"Luke, it's me, Katie. Are your parents home?"

"No."

"Neither are mine... and I have no idea where they are."

"Us too," Luke replied.

"Do you mind if we come over? I don't want to stay here all alone."

"C'mon over," Luke said.

* * *

Luke and Tommy stared out the window, waiting for Katie and Lynn to arrive. It was late, after two in the morning. Why was it taking them so long? Katie and Lynn didn't live far away, but any distance in the middle of the night can be long. By the time Luke spied them coming up the driveway, he breathed a huge sigh of relief.

"What took you so long?" he asked, darting outside and helping them bring their bags into the house.

"I had to pack a couple of things, and Lynn fell asleep," Katie explained.

No sooner had they crossed the threshold than Lynn plopped down on the floor and closed her eyes.

"Tommy can you move her upstairs to a bed?" Katie asked. She dropped her bags and collapsed onto the living room couch.

Tommy hoisted Lynn into his powerful arms and carried his cousin gently up the stairs. He tucked her into bed next to Billy and raced back down to Katie and Luke.

"So what's going on?" Katie asked. "Where are our parents?"

"They probably went on a vacation together," Tommy answered.

"I don't think so," Luke explained. "They didn't prep the house like they usually do before going away. They didn't shut off the water, there's no timer on the lights. There was milk and food in the fridge. They didn't even take their cell phones. I can't figure it out; it's like they just vanished."

"Have you checked the cameras?" Katie asked.

"What cameras?"

"You didn't know?" Katie replied. "After the big mess with your Aunt Janine at the museum, my Dad helped your Dad install security cameras."

* * *

The video was grainy, but it didn't have to be perfect for them to know what they were looking at; Aunt Janine, Abigail, No-Neck and the Walrus pulled into the driveway in Aunt Janine's limo and approached the front door. The next camera angle showed them inside the house. Mom, Dad, Uncle Brian and Aunt Eileen were there too. The next part was difficult to see because No-Neck and his extremely large frame blocked the view of the camera, but after a few minutes, the whole group exited the house with their bags packed. Where were they going? And why were they going with Aunt Janine?

42

11. Planning a Trip

Luke, Tommy and Katie sat in stunned silence. Finally, Tommy broke the pause, "So where are they?"

"I don't know, but at least we know who they're with," Luke said.

"Does that help?" Tommy replied.

"I'm not sure, but it could help us figure out where they're going."

"How?"

"I don't know," Luke said. He slumped back into Dad's overstuffed red leather chair.

"I know," Katie offered. "We do what we were planning to do all along."

"What's that?" Tommy asked.

Katie smiled. "We follow the journal. That's the best way to find your Aunt Janine."

"You can't be serious," Tommy balked. "We already tried that once and ended up right back here."

Luke's face lit up. "Katie's right. It didn't work last time, but now it'll be easier. We can make all of our arrangements from this computer and pay for it all with Dad's credit card."

A gleam came to Katie's eye. "We can arrange everything… limos, airfare, hotels."

Tommy objected, "But guys seriously, we're just kids."

Luke answered him, "If we order everything online, who's going to know we're just kids."

Tommy shook his head. "But what about when we try to check in at the airport… or when we try to check in at a hotel?"

Katie cut in, "We make the arrangements as unaccompanied minors. We won't have to fake it because we'll make sure everyone is expecting us to be alone."

"Won't someone get suspicious about three kids traveling the world all by themselves?" Tommy replied.

Luke began typing away on the computer. "It'll be five kids, don't forget Billy and Lynn," he said. "We can't leave them here all alone."

"Exactly," Tommy said, "five kids. Who's going to let five kids travel all alone?"

"I know," Katie answered. "We stay at each hotel only one night. Our story is that we're meeting our parents the very next day."

Luke pecked away at the keyboard. Soon he had flights booked to hit all of the destinations in Hans Jacobsen's journal. "How much time do you think we'll need in each city?"

"A couple of days each, I guess," Katie responded.

Tommy, still wary of the entire plan, paced back and forth. The ringing phone gave him a start. He checked the caller ID. "Uh Luke, it's the airline."

Luke looked at Katie. "Time to do your thing."

Katie grabbed the phone, took a deep breath and, in a voice that was definitely not her own, said, "Hello." She listened for a moment then responded, "Oh yes, my husband

44

was just making those arrangements, the children will be staying with relatives over the next several weeks." She paused to listen, and then added, "We've made the ground travel arrangements separately, but I assure you, one of our drivers will be there to meet them when they depart each flight."

After another extended pause, Katie said, "Thank you very much for your concern, we had a death in the family and unfortunately this situation just could not be avoided. We appreciate all of your assistance in these trying times."

12. Alpha Mission

Three thousand miles away, Abigail walked into a luxurious hotel suite wearing black spandex pants and a black form-fitting top. She pulled a black baseball cap from her head and her beautiful waves of blonde hair cascaded down to her shoulders. One flip, and her hair returned to its natural full body form.

She looked around at all the people in the room. When she spotted Uncle Al looking at her, she gave him a wink and a million dollar smile. Turning to her sister Janine she said, "Just like we thought, they have minimal security. One old guy on duty and he'll probably be asleep before we get there. But... he has a dog."

"A minor hiccup," Janine responded. She never lifted her eyes from the work on the conference table in front of her. Her mind fixated on the now familiar journal, on Soren Jacobsen, and on his precious inventions. She searched for any last clue that might have been missed, even though she had studied the text a thousand times before.

Satisfied that everything was committed to memory, she closed the journal and stood up to address the group. No-Neck and the Walrus were at the kitchen area of the hotel suite, nibbling on a plate of cheese and crackers from a catering cart. Mom, Dad, Uncle Brian and Aunt Eileen sat in a huddled circle at the far end of the room while Uncle Al sat perched on a windowsill, as nonchalant as ever. Kerri, Aunt Janine's youngest sister, sat at the conference table with her laptop open, seemingly not interested in anything her sister had to say. Abigail stood nearby.

"Will you be able to take care of the guard?" Janine asked Abigail.

"If I need to," Abigail responded. "Like I said, he'll be asleep before we even get there."

"We're not taking any chances," Janine replied. She turned to No-Neck and asked, "Are you okay with the dog?"

"No problem," No-Neck answered. Cracker crumbs spilled from his mouth. He held up a slice of prime rib from the catering cart for everyone to see and then stuffed it into the waistband of his pants.

"Kerri, you and David," Aunt Janine said pointing at The Walrus, "will watch the perimeter. You'll signal us if anyone shows up."

"I don't understand why I can't go in," Kerri protested, "I'm just as much a part of this as you are… maybe even more."

Janine glared at her youngest sister. Ever since the events in Sir Roland's chamber, their relationship had changed. "You'll do as you're told or you can stay behind. You wouldn't even be here if it wasn't for me."

Kerri raised her head as if she was about to say something, but thought better of it.

"What about us?" Mom chipped in from the far corner. "What are we going to do?"

"The four of you will wait at the perimeter until we signal that all is clear then you'll go in with us."

"Got it," Mom replied. Dad and Uncle Brian nodded their heads in agreement.

"I don't understand why I need to go," Aunt Eileen interjected. "It seems like you guys have everything covered."

"You're right," Janine responded, much to Aunt Eileen's surprise. "Why don't you stay here, out of everyone's way?"

Aunt Eileen couldn't contain her excitement. She stood up, gave Uncle Brian a kiss on the cheek and said, "I'm going to soak in that beautiful tub and take a nap, wake me when you get back."

Mom, Dad and Uncle Brian each exhaled a sigh of relief as Aunt Eileen sauntered off.

"And what job do you have for me honeybunch?" Uncle Al asked, dropping down from the windowsill and moving towards his ex wife.

"I've been trying to pretend you aren't here," Aunt Janine replied. "Now let's get ready; we have work to do."

* * *

Mom sat with Dad, Uncle Brian and Uncle Al at the edge of the cemetery, securely hidden between two bushes and the stone wall that surrounded the lot. From their location they could see the entire layout of the church, the caretaker's home and the sprawling landscape of tombstones and grave markers.

The half moon was high in the sky and provided just enough light to make out what was happening. Mom couldn't help but be amazed by the precision accuracy by which Janine's crew worked.

Abigail scurried across the lot, barely noticeable in her black outfit, hugging the shadows in her stealth approach. The guard, as Abigail had predicted, was fast asleep on a bench on the church portico. Abigail snuck up to his side and gently applied a chloroform soaked cloth to his nose and face. He struggled momentarily, but then dropped back into an unconscious state.

On the other side of the building, near the caretaker's home, No-Neck wrestled with an oversized German Shepherd. At first glance, it looked like he was in quite a battle, but upon closer inspection the large man was actually playing with the dog. After a lengthy tussle, he finally rewarded the pooch with a slab of the prime rib, taking a bite for himself before letting the canine run off with his prize.

As if on cue, Janine strolled past Kerri and The Walrus at the front gate and moved directly to the caretaker's building. She waved her hand towards Mom and the others.

"That's the signal," Mom said excitedly, "let's go." She hopped over the stone wall and took off across the cemetery.

Dad shot a knowing glance to Uncle Brian and Uncle Al. "She's a bit excited about all of this, isn't she?"

"Give her a break," Uncle Al said as he jumped over the stone wall to follow Mom. "This is her first real mission, let her enjoy it."

Uncle Brian and Dad raced to catch up. They all reached the door of the caretaker's home and entered. The building was overloaded. There were stacks of boxes, folded tents, rolled up banners, and an assortment of party supplies.

"Looks like someone's getting ready for a party," Dad commented.

"They're going to be opening this site as a tribute to Soren Jacobsen," Uncle Al explained. "They're giving tours and celebrating with a festival."

Janine glared at her ex-husband. "They wouldn't even know about it if you hadn't insisted on giving all of Soren's valuable artifacts to the museum."

"It's where it belongs," Uncle Al responded defensively. "Did you really want to keep it all for yourself?"

"In a couple of days a thousand people are going to traipse through here with no understanding of the importance of Soren Jacobsen and his work. Any chance of finding clues after that will be completely gone."

Uncle Al paused to think about Janine's comment. "I still think it was the right thing to do." He muttered the words under his breath in order to avoid antagonizing his ex-wife.

Janine ignored him. Instead, she crossed the room to the far corner where a section was cordoned off with rope. There was an old desk, a bed, and a potbelly stove next to a newly excavated hole in the floor. Makeshift steps had been constructed, leading down the hole. With a flick of a switch, Janine activated string lighting that had been installed for the grand opening.

The tunnel had been expanded and fortified in preparation for the festival. Where once they would have had to crawl fifty feet through small gaps, they were now able to walk upright along new paving stones. When they reached the end of the tunnel, they still had to squeeze through a small stone opening. Despite all of the work they had done, they didn't alter the original construction of Soren Jacobsen's entrance to the underground vault.

Everyone moved into the chamber. No-Neck immediately set to work, pulling extendable frames from the pack on his back and putting them together to form a sturdy frame. He added a few lanterns, and soon the room was flooded with light.

Mom was in awe at the sight. She had been in some of Soren Jacobsen's vaults before, in Argentina, in Denmark and in France, and while each of these was more elaborate and intricate, this one had a distinct character all its own. She immediately fell in love with the functional yet simplistic design of the dome and all of its unique alcoves.

Abigail pulled out a camera and began taking photos as fast as her finger could press the button. She was instructed to capture every last detail so that no clue would be lost. Mom saw what she was doing and decided to use her iPad to collect pictures of her own.

Dad found an interesting section of the wall and studied the inscriptions. He jotted notes as fast as he could, filling page after page in his little notebook. He seemed particularly interested in a collection of drawings that resembled Egyptian hieroglyphics. "Hon, can you come over and take pictures of these?"

Abigail hustled over before Mom had a chance to react, blocking the way and getting the best angle for photos.

"Very interesting," Dad said, jotting more notes in his notebook.

Everyone gathered around, trying to get a closer look. Janine stepped to the front of the group. "What is it?" she asked.

"I have some theories," Dad responded, "but we're going to need to see the other chambers before I can be certain."

The ringing of Janine's cell phone interrupted the conversation. "What is it?" she barked into the phone. "Okay, how many and where are they?" She listened and then hung up. "Gather your things, we have company."

* * *

Back in the hotel suite, Aunt Eileen settled into a hot bath, overflowing with white bubbles. Scented candles gave the room a soft glimmering glow and a fragrance of eucalyptus and vanilla now permeated the suite. She pulled a sleep mask over her eyes and laid back, allowing the foaming bubbles to envelope her body. Time seemed to stand still; the combination of soothing bath oils and warm water slowly took its effect.

As much as she wanted to relax, she couldn't. Her mind kept returning to the group and their mission to unearth the secrets of Soren Jacobsen. That was weird. She hadn't much cared about any of the details of this trip before, why was it consuming her mind right now? She tried to wipe away the thoughts, concentrating instead on the relaxing pool of comfort.

There it was again, that pesky thought. No matter how hard she tried, she couldn't help but feel that she was missing out on something, something unique and important. The decision came to her all of a sudden. She wanted, *no needed*, to be a part of the adventure. It was time to pick herself out of the comfort and security of her predictable life, and her comfortable bath, and become a part of the excitement.

In one fluid motion, she jumped from the tub, grabbed her robe from the hook on the bathroom door, and headed for her suitcase. The stylish adventure outfits she'd purchased for this trip were there, waiting for her.

She rifled through the stacks of clothes. As she contemplated what to wear, she noticed a strange musky scent in the air. Before she could figure out what it was, a hand wrapped across her mouth and a strong, hairy arm grappled her waist. Her body flipped and she landed hard on the bed. Her voice never had the chance to render the scream that was surging through her terrified mind. A man with black eyes and scraggly hair pinned her down. He used one hand to secure her mouth and the other to hold her arms above her head. The stench of his breath attacked her nostrils. He spat in her face. "Stay where you are and don't make a sound."

Aunt Eileen's heart raced. She tried to take in what was happening. What was going on? Why was she being terrorized? What was he going to do to her? The room was dimly lit, but she could make out a jagged white scar on the side of his olive toned cheek. His powerful arms pinned her effortlessly, and his eyes held a cold menace, detached from human emotion.

She couldn't stop the tears; they streamed down her face. She tried to stay calm, but the situation was too much. Only moments ago she was wanting more adventure in her life, but now all she could think was how much she wished she was back in the comfort of the warm bath.

Another voice echoed in the room. For a moment, her fears allayed. There was hope, someone to help. But the sounds were unintelligible, the words foreign. The terror returned, as real as ever. The man on top of her looked in her eyes and shouted, "Where is the journal?"

"What?" she managed to reply through gasps and tears. It took a moment for her mind to process what he was saying. "The journal? I don't know. You can have it... They took it, to the chamber. Please, just don't hurt me."

The other voice in the room blurted more unrecognizable words, and the man turned on her once again. If she thought before that his cold black eyes could show no emotion then she was wrong, because right now, as he dominated over her, she could see his anger, an inner rage that did not bode well for what might happen next.

Despite having a husband who was one of the premier martial arts instructors in the world, Aunt Eileen had never taken much interest in self-defense. If she had, then she might have been able to strike a blow or even inflict some harm. But, as it were, she was unable to free herself, nor was she able to stop the chloroform covered rag that was forced over her nose and mouth. All of her senses blacked out, as did the world around her.

* * *

Back at the chamber, Janine's crew bolted into action. In a matter of moments, No-Neck had dismantled the lighting system and stowed it in his pack. Abigail finished taking her photos, and together the three of them filed out through the tunnel and back to the caretaker's cabin.

Mom, Dad, Uncle Brian and Uncle Al watched the efficiency in awe, and then followed. When they reached the main room of the caretaker's building, Janine was there to direct them.

"Lena, you and John ," Aunt Janine said to Mom and Dad, "you stay to the rear. Brian, it's time for you to show off your skills. There are four men approaching the entrance in two by two formation. They're armed and look like they have military experience. You take out the two to the left, Abigail and Elliott will handle the men on the right." Abigail and No-Neck nodded at Aunt Janine's words, readying themselves for the fight.

Uncle Brian asked, "Do we even know who they are? Do they mean to attack us?"

"They're not in a cemetery in the middle of the night because they want to have a picnic," Janine mocked.

"Maybe they're here for the same reason we are," Uncle Brian answered.

"They *are* here for the same reason we are, to learn Soren Jacobsen's secrets," Janine replied, "only they're trained professionals. They're here to do a job, and nothing and no one is going to stand in their way."

Uncle Brian looked to Mom and Dad, and then to Uncle Al. "We hide behind those boxes and let them pass right by us," he said. "Once they're inside the chamber, we escape."

"That's your big plan?" Janine gasped, "to hide?"

55

"There's no reason anyone has to get hurt."

Janine rolled her eyes, but realizing her plan wasn't going to work without him, she instructed Abigail and No-Neck to follow his lead. "Get behind those tents on this side," she directed, "let them hide on that side."

Everyone took their positions and waited. It seemed like an eternity. Every creek of a floorboard and every beat of their hearts was magnified in the waiting silence. Finally, they heard something at the door.

It was the sound of a man picking the lock. Had he thought to try the knob, he would have found that Janine and her crew never locked it when they entered. Either way, it only took him a moment, and the door was open. Four men dressed in black entered the room, outfitted in full combat gear, their faces covered with scarves. They closed the door behind them, and then lit the room with their flashlights.

Mom's nerves overwhelmed her. One of the men was so close she could touch him. Sweat dripped from her brow, her heart raced. They were going to get caught; she knew it. Her hands shook uncontrollably.

13. First Stop France

The plane carrying Luke and the others landed at the Paris airport, an airline agent was there to greet them as they got off. "Good evening," she said with only the slightest hint of a French accent, "I will be happy to escort you to your guardian."

"We have to grab our bags and meet our driver," Luke explained to the woman. Together they headed towards baggage claim and, in a voice meant only for Katie, Luke whispered, "According to the journal, the first of the pieces was hidden in a small town near Normandy."

"How far is that?" Katie questioned. "These guys are pretty tired." She nodded towards Billy and Lynn. The pair of them struggled to stay upright, staggering from exhaustion.

"I told everyone to get some rest on the flight," Luke scolded.

"They're kids," Katie laughed. "They don't listen."

"We have to make it to Rouen," Luke replied. "We're staying in a hotel there tonight and then we'll head to the cemetery in the morning."

They moved towards the baggage claim area where they spotted a man in a black suit holding a sign that read, "Stolin."

The airline agent addressed the man, "I understand you will be transporting the children to their hotel?"

The man nodded.

"May I see some identification?"

He nodded again and flashed a badge attached to his belt.

"Very well," the woman said and, turning to Luke and the others she said, "Farewell children, I hope you enjoy your visit to France."

Luke waved the woman off and then whispered to Katie and the others, "Remember, we're meeting our parents at the hotel." He needed to remind everyone of the story they had concocted to explain their travel arrangement.

Tommy approached the driver. "Bonsoir Monsieur," he said. "Nous sommes les Stolins."

"Bonsoir," the driver replied. "Hotel de Bourgtheroulde in Rouen. Vous avez des luggage?"

Tommy motioned to the conveyor belt. "They should be coming down soon.

The driver eyed the bag draped over Luke's shoulder. Luke clutched it tight beneath his arm.

It took a while for the bags to arrive from the airplane and in that time Luke, Katie and Tommy discussed their plans. They didn't notice the little ones wander away.

First, Billy and Lynn explored the bathrooms, and then the lost baggage counter, and eventually they found the luggage conveyor. Lynn crawled on all fours, up the tunnel and into the chute. Billy was right behind, scurrying to keep up.

Inside, they found a collection of luggage from their flight. Lynn searched through the piles, tossing bags aside, this way and that, until she found what she was looking for, her pink bag with flowers on the side. She tore at the zipper until she managed to open the compartment. She grinned from ear to ear when she found her special teddy bear. She hugged the bear and settled to rest in the center of the bag.

Billy rifled through the remaining bags, tossing suitcases over the rail and down onto the floor. When he was done, only five bags remained: Lynn's, Katie's and the three belonging to Luke, Tommy and himself. He opened the first and searched within. He did the same with the second and then the third until he found what he was looking for, his special blankie. He rubbed the soft blankie against his face and smiled a contented smile, putting his head down on a pile of clothes and falling fast asleep.

* * *

All the people waiting for their luggage gathered at the bottom of the chute. A couple of businessmen moved to the front, anxious to retrieve their bags. A group of teenagers, travelling as a group, jockeyed for position. A pair of fathers moved closer while their wives and children backed away from the fracas. Luke, Tommy and Katie were unable to get anywhere close. The limo driver was no help at all. He chose to stay away from the waiting crowd.

A buzzer sounded. Everyone rushed to the conveyor like pigs to the feeding trough. The belt began to move, but no luggage appeared. Several minutes passed, but still no bags. People began to murmur and complain until one piece of luggage came through the chute, followed by four more. The first was an oversized pink backpack with flowers on the side and a small girl bundled in the center. The next bags were opened, their contents scattered along the conveyor belt. The last of the bags was wide open, a small boy curled up inside.

The crowd watched in stunned silence as the bags and the children made their way down the chute and onto the platform. Every eye watched and waited for more bags, but there were none.

Sheepishly, Katie stepped forward, gathered all of her loose clothes and shoved them back inside her backpack. She roused Lynn from her slumber in the process. Luke and Tommy did the same with their bags, forcing Billy out of his backpack and onto the floor.

Luke whispered to Katie, "Let's get out of here before everyone figures out what happened."

Katie was one step ahead of him, dragging two bags toward the limo driver and guiding Lynn along the way. Luke and Tommy were close behind, carrying three backpacks and Billy, in an effort to get out of the airport as quickly as possible.

"We're ready," Luke told the driver, "let's get going."

The driver looked past Luke at the angry crowd. He gave the kids a disgruntled grimace before leading them out of the building.

* * *

The van pulled up in front of the Hotel de Bourgtheroulde, a magnificent building, very old and very impressive. The first thing Luke noticed was the detail of the stonework and the spires jetting into the sky. Then he saw the intricate archway that led to the front lobby. It had so many decorative features it was hard to decide what to look at first. Everything drew his eye to a blue shield above the archway, flanked by two lions standing on their hind legs, like they were showcasing the shield for all to see.

The driver helped the kids out of the van and then moved to the back where he pulled their luggage off of the vehicle and placed it on the red carpet that lined the sidewalk. When the last bag was out, he looked at Luke expectantly, his hand extended.

Luke froze, not sure what to do.

Katie stepped forward, "Your tip was included when our parents booked your service," she said in a mature and admonishing tone.

The driver grunted and turned away. The van was gone before the kids had a chance to enter the hotel.

Luke looked to Katie. "Are you ready for this?"

It was agreed that Katie would do the talking when they checked in. She drew in a deep breath. "I've got this," she said with a smile. She turned on her heel, strutted through the doors, marched through the hotel lobby and across to the registration counter. If Luke didn't know better, he would have thought she owned the place. People stopped and stared, but it didn't faze her one bit.

An attractive young woman stood behind the counter. She had brown curly hair that hung loosely around her face. Her broad rimmed glasses matched the decorative piping on her crisp hotel uniform. Katie approached and addressed her in her most mature voice, "Excuse me, you there." Her words had a pompous flare to them. "I believe you have a reservation for our party, the Stolins."

61

The woman was speechless. She looked Katie up and down, surprised that the words that came from Katie's mouth did not match the visage before her.

"Is there a problem?" Katie asked, her tone authoritative and slightly condescending. "We've been traveling all day and the little ones are quite tired."

"Ver are zee parents?" the woman finally managed to ask.

"I believe this has all been arranged," Katie told her. "You should have it all in your computer." Katie was good at this; she had such confidence she was beginning to believe the story herself.

It took a moment for the woman behind the counter to collect herself, but once she did, and she looked up the reservation on the computer, her attitude changed. "I'm very sorry Mademoiselle Stolin, you are correct… I zee your parents vill be meeting tomorrow. Shall I arrange to have someone look in on you later this evening?"

"That won't be necessary," Katie replied. "We've had a long flight and the little ones need their rest. It would be best if we had some peace and quiet."

"Of course," the woman responded dutifully. "I will zee to it that you are not disturbed." She handed over two key cards along with some information about the hotel. "All of zee charges will be billed to zee credit card on file," the woman explained. "Your room is number 423, take zee elevator to zee third level, then go down zee hall to your left."

"Thank you," Katie said. She took the keys and motioned everyone toward the elevator.

Everyone clambered after Katie, dragging their bags close behind. Tommy waited until the elevator doors shut before saying, "You were incredible, I never could have kept a straight face through all of that."

Katie's face turned into a broad, gushing smile. "It's all about confidence and attitude," she explained. "If *you* believe it, you can make *them* believe it."

They got off the elevator and walked down the corridor to room number 423. Katie swiped her key and opened the door. When they entered the room, Tommy ran over and jumped on top of one of the beds. Billy and Lynn fell onto the other bed and were asleep as soon as their heads hit the pillow.

Luke leaned his backpack against the wall and dropped his carry-on bag on the ground in front of the little refrigerator. "We should fill our backpacks with the food from the minibar," he said. "Where's the key?"

"I forgot to ask for the key to the minibar," Katie replied sheepishly.

Luke's reaction showed his disappointment. "We need it!" he stated matter-of-factly. "We need to conserve our cash as much as possible; that food is important."

Katie's jaw dropped, and tears started to form in her eyes. She ran into the bathroom and slammed the door.

Luke turned to Tommy. "We need to go over the schedule for tomorrow."

"Are you kidding me?" Tommy balked.

"What?"

"Didn't you just see Katie?"

"She went into the bathroom, what's the big deal?"

No," Tommy explained, "she ran into the bathroom because of you."

"What are you talking about?"

"Didn't you see how upset she was?"

"Why would she be upset?"

"You don't get it. She just smooth-talked that woman downstairs, got us into the room with no adult and no questions, and all you could do was bark at her for not getting a key to the minibar."

Katie peaked her head out of the bathroom.

"It's okay Katie," Luke told her, "you can go back down and get the key."

Katie retreated back inside the bathroom and slammed the door. Tommy grunted and shrugged.

14. Best Laid Plans

The men in the black military attire scanned the caretaker's cabin. The beam from one of the flashlights passed over the box that Mom and the others were hiding behind. Something caught his attention and he moved closer.

Mom's hands shook uncontrollably, she couldn't keep still; the stress was too much. Her anxious nerves caused her entire body to vibrate, her breathing shortened and her head felt dizzy. She was going to pass out and there wasn't anything she could do about it. One more step and his foot would bump into her. She tried to think. What could she do?

On the opposite side of the room Abigail and No-Neck watched what was happening. They moved towards the other men. This was all about to go bad real quick. No-Neck raised his bag filled with the lighting gear and prepared to strike.

As if on cue, one of the men called out, "Over here!" The men lowered their flashlights and moved away from Mom and towards the chamber entrance. The four men scurried into the tunnel.

No sooner had the last man passed the threshold than Janine led Abigail and No-Neck out the door and into the cool night air. Uncle Brian directed Mom, Dad and Uncle Al towards the door, but Mom was rooted to the spot, unable to get herself to move. With Dad on one side and Uncle Al on the other, they grabbed her by the arms and shuttled her out of the building. Uncle Brian brought up the rear, making sure they weren't followed. He gently closed the door behind them.

Together, they raced to catch up with Janine and her crew at the entrance to the cemetery where Kerri and The Walrus were waiting with the van, ready to make a quick departure.

* * *

Riding away from the cemetery and back to the hotel, the van bubbled with excitement. For Mom and Dad, it was the adrenalin from the near conflict and the nifty escape. For Aunt Janine, it was the added knowledge that came from Dad's discovery of the murals on the chamber wall. Either way, the inside of the van was buzzing with an electric energy.

"I'm glad Eileen wasn't there," Uncle Brian said. "I can only imagine how she would have reacted when those men came in."

"Tell me about it," Mom said, "she would've freaked."

"Look who's talking," Dad laughed, "you weren't exactly the picture of calm, cool and collected."

Mom gave him a playful punch on the arm. "Those guys had guns; anything could have happened in there."

Aunt Janine, who had remained relatively quiet until now, said, "We have to learn from this, Yousef and his men are closer than we thought. When we get back to the hotel we need to pack up and move on. We can't risk them getting ahead of us."

"So who were those men?" Dad asked. "Are they followers of Soren Jacobsen as well?"

Aunt Janine went silent. She looked at Abigail and then Kerri with long meaningful stares.

Finally, Abigail broke the silence. "There're a lot of people who are searching for clues about Soren Jacobsen and his inventions, but no one has gotten as far as we have."

"But who were those men?" Uncle Brian asked. "Is that the guy who attacked Tommy and Luke at the karate tournament?"

"It's hard to explain about Yousef," Abigail answered. "Let's just say he's coming at this thing from a different angle."

Dad had more questions, but he didn't get a chance to voice them. They pulled into the garage beneath the hotel, and in a flash, Aunt Janine and her crew were ushering everyone out of the van and into the elevator. "We need everything packed and ready to go in fifteen minutes."

At the top floor, the elevator doors opened and everyone hustled down the hallway. Just like in the cemetery, Aunt Janine's crew moved with precision accuracy and determined purpose.

They hadn't reached the door to the suite and everyone already knew that something was wrong. The door was ajar and, from what they could see, the room had been tossed.

Aunt Janine signaled silently to her crew. They followed her wordless directions, and in a matter of moments they stormed the room, prepared for whatever may lie within.

There was nothing to find. The suite had been searched, everything had been disturbed, but no one was left behind, not even Aunt Eileen. Uncle Brian ran about, searching for clues as to what had happened and where his wife could be. He was in a panic.

Aunt Janine did not seem surprised that the room had been breached, nor did she seem concerned that Aunt Eileen was gone. Instead, she instructed her team, "Gather your things and make it quick."

"Eileen's gone!" Uncle Brian shouted. "What happened to her?"

"You realize the men you didn't want to hurt back at the cemetery are the same ones that took your wife?" Janine said to him.

Uncle Brian was caught between consuming worry and raging anger. He stared daggers at Janine. "Are you just going to gloat and say 'I told you so' or are you going to help?"

"If you're asking if I'm going to go after a group of mercenaries to get your wife back, the answer is *no*. It's a fool's errand that will only end in bloodshed."

"After all we've done for you?" Uncle Brian asked, incredulously. "Back at the cemetery you were ready to have me destroy them."

"Back at the cemetery we were cornered and I thought it was the best way to get us all out safely. Besides," Janine laughed, "you haven't really done that much for me... I'm doing all of this as a favor to you."

"We're talking about my wife... we need to do something." Uncle Brian was exasperated. He needed to do

68

something, but it was obvious Janine and her resources would not be available to help.

"I understand your loyalty, it's really admirable. But what good would all of us getting captured, or worse, really do?"

Uncle Brian's frustration grew. "You're not going to do anything?"

"I wouldn't say that," Janine responded. "I'm going to move on to our next destination. We have a mission and an agenda, and this location has been compromised." She turned to the members of her crew. "Pack your things; we leave in five minutes."

Mom stepped forward. "We're not going anywhere without Eileen."

"Suit yourself," Janine responded. Abigail and Kerri had their bags packed and were ready to leave; No-Neck and The Walrus were busy collecting the last of their belongings.

Uncle Brian stopped Janine before she reached the door. "You can at least tell us where we can find them."

Janine looked him up and down then said, "If you hurry, you can still catch them at the chamber. After that, it's anyone's guess where they'll go."

And with that, she and her crew raced out the door and down the hallway. When they got to the elevator, Janine turned to Kerri and said, "Tell the front desk to have them out of the suite within the hour."

"We still need them, don't we?" Abigail asked.

"You're right," Janine responded. "Keep tabs on them and make sure they find their way back to us."

* * *

Back in the room, Uncle Brian grabbed his and Aunt Eileen's bags and headed for the door.

Mom stopped him. "Brian, we need to at least have a plan."

"We don't have time, every moment we waste they could be gone," he answered. He tried to step around his sister.

Uncle Al stepped forward. "She's right Brian, we can't just storm the cemetery. You saw what kind of fire power they have; it could get us all killed."

Dad cut in, "Brian's right, we need to get moving. We can talk about a plan on the way. We're going to have to walk since Janine is the one with the van."

They formulated a plan on the walk over to the cemetery, but it went completely out the window when they ducked between the bushes and the cemetery wall, looked over, and saw six men milling around the front of the caretaker's building. To make matters worse, the night guard, who had been knocked unconscious by Abigail and her chloroform rag, was now tied and gagged. These men meant business, and they weren't going to let anyone stand in their way.

"I think the plan will still work," Uncle Brian said confidently. He mentally prepared himself for an aggressive confrontation.

"You're kidding yourself," Dad said. "We need to come up with a new plan; there are six men there, and who knows how many more inside. Besides, we're not even sure if Eileen is with them."

Uncle Brian didn't want to hear it. "If she's not with them, they'll know where she is. I'm going whether you help or not."

Mom cut in, "We're not saying we're not going to help, we just have to be smart about this."

"I'll take out all six guys," Uncle Brian said. "You don't have to do anything."

"Even if you could take all out six guys," Dad replied, "what do you think is waiting for us inside the building?"

"We'll worry about that after we take out the first six," Uncle Brian answered, impatiently. "I can't wait any longer; can you guys provide a distraction or not?"

Mom saw the look in her brother's eyes and sensed his despair. She couldn't disappoint him. With a nod, she gave him her consent. He was off. Mom and Dad stayed hidden in the bushes while Uncle Brian circled around the church and snuck up behind the group of men.

"It's time," she said to Dad. "Are you ready?"

"As ready as I'll ever be," Dad replied.

Together, they walked to the front gate and down the main driveway, directly towards the group of men and the caretaker's cabin. "Aaaahhh," Mom wailed, burying her head on Dad's shoulder, "pourquoi a t'elle besoin de mourir?"

The men noticed the couple walking into the cemetery and watched as Mom and Dad got about three quarters of the way down the path and then turned into a row of grave sites.

Mom wailed out again, "Mon bébé! Pourquoi avez-vous pris mon bébé?"

Three of the men left the group and moved towards Mom and Dad who were now crying over a freshly placed grave.

Uncle Brian used the distraction to sneak up behind the remaining men. He unleashed a lightning quick combination of kicks and punches. The first two men dropped to the ground after blows to the head, the third man was incapacitated by a headlock and a sharp jab of the thumb to a pressure point just below his left ear.

Thirty feet away, the other men approached Mom and Dad. "Que faites-vous ici?" one of the men asked. "Le cimetière est fermé."

Mom cried out, "Mon bébé!"

The men looked at one another, bewildered by what to do with this couple grieving over the loss of their baby. As they debated their options, Uncle Brian crept closer. He wrapped his powerful arms around the first man's head and, in a matter of seconds, dropped him, unconscious, to the ground. The other men tried to react. The first was met with a sharp jab to the throat, the second a kick to the jaw. Both lay on the ground, unable to move.

"That was incredible Brian," Dad said, amazed by the extraordinary demonstration of martial arts moves.

"That *was* incredible," a voice said from the darkness. Before they had a chance to react, a group of armed men surrounded them and a tall, dark skinned man emerged from the shadows. His straggly black hair blew in the breeze, and the moonlight reflected off of the jagged scar that ran down the left side of his face. "I have never seen you in action, but

I saw your student at the karate tournament last year. He would have won had he not interfered with me."

Mom, Dad and Uncle Brian looked on in disbelief.

* * *

Uncle Al stood at the front gate watching the turn of events. He knew there was only one thing left to do. He started up the main driveway when a voice from behind stopped him in his tracks.

"Where do you think you're going?"

Uncle Al turned to see Abigail come out from behind a couple of bushes. "What are you doing here?" he asked.

"I came to keep you from doing something stupid, and it looks like I got here just in time. Where do you think you're going?"

"I got them into this mess," Uncle Al replied. "I need to get them out."

"By committing suicide?" Abigail responded.

"They won't kill me," Uncle Al answered.

"What makes you think that?" Abigail said.

"Because I have something that they want."

Abigail shook her head. "Janine has the journal."

"I have all of the information up here," he said, tapping his forefinger to his temple.

"And you think you can just tell them and everything will be fine?"

"I'll trade myself and lead them to a couple of chambers and then, somewhere along the way, I'll ditch them."

"You're not going alone," Abigail said to him.

Uncle Al nodded his consent and together they walked down the main drive of the cemetery.

The group that was gathered around Mom, Dad and Uncle Brian at the gravesite stopped what they were doing and watched as the pair approached.

"Hey," Uncle Al called out. With his usual casual charm he added, "I was wondering if we might see you guys here."

Yousef's men spread out to allow Uncle Al and Abigail to enter the group, their guns still directed firmly at Uncle Brian, Mom and Dad. "Glad you could join us," Yousef said.

"I'm here to broker a deal," Uncle Al replied. "You can have me, but you have to let them go."

"I don't want you, I want the journal," Yousef replied. "Unless you have it in that bag, then no deal."

"I have what you're looking for, but it's not in my bag. I have it all up here." Uncle Al tapped his noggin as he said it.

"How do I know you're telling the truth?"

Uncle Al laughed. "You know who I am. I've been where you want to go."

"And you'll take us there?" Yousef asked skeptically.

"I will if you let them go," Uncle Al answered.

Yousef looked around at Mom, Dad and Uncle Brian. He motioned to his men.

Uncle Al interrupted, "And Eileen too," he added.

Yousef raised his hand and waved towards the caretaker's cabin. Another armed man emerged, dragging

74

Aunt Eileen behind him. As soon as she saw Uncle Brian, she shrieked and ran to him. She wrapped him in a hug and broke down in tears.

Yousef pointed at Uncle Al and Abigail. "Get those two," he said. "And let the others go."

Uncle Al protested, "Just me, leave her out of this."

"I want more leverage than that; either she comes or they all come."

"It's okay," Abigail said. "I'll go."

Mom, Dad, Uncle Brian and Aunt Eileen shuffled way from the men and towards the cemetery entrance. As Mom passed her, Abigail whispered, "Stick to the itinerary and you can still catch up with them."

As soon as Mom and the others were clear of the cemetery, Yousef turned to Uncle Al and Abigail. "They're gone, now it's time to share what you know."

Uncle Al looked around at the group. Most of the men were dressed in black fatigues with scarves over their faces. Several were pointing their guns at him, and the other half at Abigail. Understandably, most of the men were gawking at Abigail's beauty. For once in her life, she actually seemed unnerved by the attention.

"If you really want to learn all about Soren Jacobsen, then we are going to have to go to Argentina," Uncle Al said.

"Who are you kidding?" Yousef laughed. "That's just a distraction to lead us off the track and get us away from here."

"I wish it were," Uncle Al responded, "but Argentina is where it all begins. It has way more information than you'll find at any of the locations like this." Uncle Al pointed to the caretaker's cabin.

Yousef had already been inside and was obviously underwhelmed by what he found. "So where in Argentina?"

"Just outside of Buenos Aires," Uncle Al said.

Abigail shot him a glance.

Yousef stepped towards her. "So there really is something in Argentina?" He looked into her eyes, and for a moment seemed to get lost in her beauty. He broke from his momentary trance. "Let's go to South America." He turned to walk away, but before he did, he added, "Cover her face; she's too much of a distraction."

The men nudged Uncle Al with their guns, directing him to follow Yousef. Then they put a scarf over Abigail's head and forced her to follow.

15. First Site

Luke and the others were giddy. The excitement was palpable. They were on their way to the first of Soren Jacobsen's secret chambers. Public transportation would only take them so far; after that it was a short walk to the cemetery and the caretaker's cabin. Hans Jacobsen's journal was leading them, just like it had led Uncle Al and Aunt Janine so many years ago. There was a magical feeling in the air. They got off of the bus and crossed the town square. Katie and Tommy were as excited as Luke. Billy and Lynn were more interested in the various stores and side streets they passed along the way.

Each of them had their own expectations about what they would encounter when they reached the graveyard, but none of them could have predicted what they found.

It was a circus, both literally and figuratively. There were people everywhere. Not just a couple here and a couple there, but crowds and crowds of people as far as the eye could see. And it wasn't just the people, but there was a band, and clowns, and even a man in a top hat with a megaphone.

"What's going on here? Why would so many people be hanging out in a cemetery?" Katie asked.

"Maybe it's like the Day of the Dead, where people celebrate the lives of everyone who has passed away," Luke offered.

Tommy grabbed Billy and Lynn and pulled them in. "We better keep these two close."

"Uh, Luke," Katie stammered. "Look."

77

On the opposite side of the cemetery, above a large colorful tent, a banner swung in the breeze. Neither Luke nor Katie could read any of the words with the exception of two: "Soren Jacobsen."

"Hey look," Tommy pointed. "They've turned this into a shrine for Soren Jacobsen. This must be some kind of celebration to mark the grand opening."

The kids forged their way through the crowd, Luke and Katie at the front, and Tommy, corralling Billy and Lynn, brought up the rear. Even though they didn't speak the language, it was obvious this was a celebration. Laughter, smiles and joyous music are universal after all.

"So where do you think the caretaker's house is?" Tommy asked, trying to be heard over the cacophony of sounds.

Luke pointed at the large multi-colored tent. "All of the festivities seem to lead there."

From the outside it had all the appearances of a big top circus, but inside it looked like a diorama that you might see in a museum, one of those staged settings that tell you all about what life was like back in the day. The settings were usually an old schoolhouse or a pioneer's cabin but, in this case, it was the inside of a caretaker's quarters.

A cot sat in the corner, a dresser with a mirror, an old razor, a wooden bowl and a pitcher on top. Opposite the dresser stood a small potbelly stove, and next to it, a big opening in the floor with a neon arrow right above, pointing down. Uncle Al had described it as a narrow tunnel beneath loosened floorboards, but it was a lot different now. With a steady stream of people traipsing through, the environment was completely changed. Luke headed for the opening, but was stopped by an older woman with an apron around her waist and a cup in her hand.

"5 euros par personne," the woman said. With a point of her crooked finger towards Billy and Lynn, she added, "pour les petits, c'est gratuits."

Dumfounded, Luke stopped in his tracks. He had no idea what this woman wanted and when he tried to go around her, she stepped in front of him, rattled her cup and repeated, "5 euros par personne."

"She wants money," Tommy explained. "5 euros... there's an admission to go in."

The woman took one look at Tommy and her disposition changed. She reached her wrinkly hand toward him and touched his surfer blonde hair. Her eyes showed longing and admiration, and then in a soft voice whispered, "Vous pouvez aller." She pointed towards the opening and motioned for Tommy to proceed.

Tommy stepped by the woman and into the hole. Billy and Lynn scampered in right behind him. Luke tried to follow, but she stopped him and said, "5 euros."

Reluctantly, Luke pulled some money from his pocket and paid for Katie and himself. The old woman handed him a brochure from her apron and gestured that he could pass. With a nod towards one another, they entered the hallowed ground that Soren Jacobsen had built and Uncle Al had once followed.

16. The First Museum

The walkway was once a tunnel, but had been retrofitted with paving stones and string lighting to accommodate tourists. It sloped downward for about 100 feet and then there was a small opening to a circular room about 25 feet across. Electric lights were set-up where once candelabras had provided the only source of light. They were alone inside the chamber. Apparently few people at the festival were willing to pay the admission.

"Do you recognize the domed ceiling?" Luke asked, pointing at the incredible architectural feat. "It says here," he said, reading aloud from the brochure, "that he used domes because it was the best structure to support the weight of the dirt above."

Katie was too busy snapping photos to listen. Tommy chased Billy and Lynn, who were scampering in and out of the small cabinet-like alcoves that surrounded the room.

"So where do you think Uncle Al found the lever?" Luke asked. He waited for an answer, but no one was paying attention to him. He decided to look for himself.

The chamber had a lot of little nooks; perfect little compartments to house and display the unique contraptions Soren Jacobsen invented. Most of them were empty right now, except for two that held glass display cases. Luke imagined that when Uncle Al and Aunt Janine were first here, each of the alcoves was filled with interesting objects. "According to the brochure," Luke said to no one in particular, "some of the items are on display in the cases, but most were either looted or taken to more prominent museums."

As Luke took a closer look around, he realized that there was more to this room than just the artifacts in the display cases. There were other remains from Soren Jacobsen's time, less obvious remnants that could not be removed because they were built right into the structure itself. Within each area there were markings on the wall, odd symbols and shapes that at first glance could have been natural imperfections in the stone, but upon further inspection were definitely man made, designed with a purpose, probably by Soren Jacobsen himself.

"What could they mean?" Luke pondered. He felt the stone with his fingers. "Is it some kind of language?" Luke turned to Katie to ask her to photograph the images, but he didn't need to, she was already focusing her lens and snapping away.

One symbol caught Luke's eye. It was a slanted line with a serpentine vine wrapped around it. Luke found this symbol in several locations, repeated in a strange, yet meaningful, pattern. It meant something, Luke was certain, but what, he wasn't sure. Another symbol showed three flags: one black, one white and one green. The vibrancy of the color was incredible.

There were several other symbols, some that Luke knew, and others that he didn't. If only he could decipher what they meant.

"Luke look," Katie called out. Luke rushed over to where Katie was taking pictures. "I think this is where your Uncle Al found the lever."

"What makes you so sure?" Luke asked.

"Look," she pointed, "see the marking, it looks just like the lever Uncle Al described."

Luke looked closer, the resemblance was undeniable, and there, next to the image of the lever was the same symbol from before, the slanted line with the serpentine vine around it. Luke knew he had seen this image before, but where? He couldn't quite place it.

Luke read from the brochure. "One of the museums where many of the inventions were moved is in Italy," he said. "I think we need to check it out." He looked around, but no one was listening; Katie was taking more photos and Tommy was wrestling with Billy and Lynn.

"Sure Luke," Luke said sarcastically, "that's a great idea, thanks for thinking of it."

17. Argentina Once Again

The flight from Paris to Buenos Aires is long, fourteen hours. Yousef and his men traveled in the main compartment of the private jet while Uncle Al and Abigail were handcuffed and secured in a baggage compartment below.

Abigail pulled the scarf from her face as soon as they were alone. "How do women breathe in these things?"

"That's the least of our worries right now," Uncle Al responded.

Abigail looked at him with concern in her eyes. "I know you wanted to get him as far away from the others as possible, but are we really taking them to the chamber?"

"We're going to have to show him something, and the chamber in Argentina has a lot to show," Uncle Al answered.

"Aren't you worried about what he'll find?"

"I think he knows most of it anyway. You know which side he's on. It'll give him information, but not the answers."

Abigail went silent, pondering all of the possibilities of what could happen to them.

Uncle Al interrupted her thinking. "So why did you come back to the cemetery? Janine made it clear she didn't want to."

"I couldn't leave you alone," Abigail responded, catching his attention and holding his gaze in her big blue eyes. "You know I have a thing for you... always have."

Uncle Al laughed. "I was married to your sister."

"It wasn't supposed to be like that," Abigail answered. "It was supposed to be me who went to the soup kitchen in Philly and made friends with Lena."

"So why wasn't it?"

"Because of you," Abigail said, breaking the eye contact and looking down at her feet. "When we were scouting you, Janine knew I felt too much."

"What?"

"When we were checking you out," Abigail explained. "We had been watching Lena and John. And every time I reported on you, she said I couldn't stop blushing."

"Get outta here," Uncle Al replied.

"Like you didn't know," Abigail laughed. "You knew the first time we met. I could tell. I felt it."

"Why didn't you ever say anything?"

"Yeah," Abigail said with a guffaw, "to my sister's husband… who was part of our scheme. How would that have gone over?"

"You've had some time since then," Uncle Al said.

"Not really," Abigail replied. "Either someone is there or the timing wasn't right." She held up her hands and shook the handcuffs.

"So why tell me now?"

"We're alone, and…" she shook her handcuffs again, "this may be the last chance I get."

Uncle Al went silent.

"So are you gonna tell me?" Abigail asked.

"Tell you what?"

"Do you like me?"

"There isn't a man on the planet that doesn't like you," Uncle Al responded, adding a trademark wink. "That's not what I mean," Abigail said. "Do you feel the connection that I feel?" Uncle Al didn't get a chance to respond. The hatch at the end of the compartment flew open and two men streamed in. They grabbed Uncle Al by both arms and hoisted him up off the floor. Abigail tried to protest, but before she could say anything, one of the men grabbed the scarf from the floor and put it back over her head. By the time she wrestled it off, they were gone.

18. Mama Mia

Luke's pre-planned itinerary included a trip on the night train, Artesia. They boarded at the Gare de Bercy train station exactly as planned, and entered their private couchette. It had a portal window, a small stainless steel bath, and six bunk-beds, a confined space, but enough sleeping room for all of them.

The Artesia line takes a little over fourteen hours to get from Paris to Rome. Luke and the others slept for almost ten of those hours, pacified by the rumble of the rails and the peace of the secure cabin. When morning came, they enjoyed a nice breakfast of croissants, yogurt, and strawberries while overlooking the beautiful scenery of southern France.

By late afternoon they were off of the train and making their way to UNA Hotel Roma. It was a short walk, and in true Katie-like fashion, she had them checked in with the receptionist, and had their room keys and a collection of area brochures in no time.

* * *

"This is the life," Tommy said in the hotel room. He put his feet on the coffee table, leaned back in the recliner, and stretched his arms high above his head. He grabbed the TV remote and flipped through the channels.

Luke slapped his feet off the table. "We're not on vacation; we have a job to do."

"Chill out," Tommy replied, "it's almost eight o'clock. We're not going anywhere until tomorrow morning; let's relax tonight. Maybe we should go down to the pool."

"We'll have plenty of time to relax later. Right now we need to go over our schedule."

Tommy put his feet back on the table. "You go over the plan. I'm gonna relax. You know what they say, 'Why do today what you can put off 'til tomorrow?'"

"That's now what they say," Luke answered.

Katie saw the frustration growing on Luke. She stepped between her cousins and offered, "Just let him relax, I'll go over the schedule with you."

"Relax, Luke," Tommy said, "you need to enjoy the moments we get... recharge your battery. You don't know when we're going to get another chance to kick back and take it easy."

Luke and Katie laid out the brochures they had picked up in the lobby. Katie opened the first pamphlet. "Don't get too comfortable Tommy," she laughed, "the museum is open tonight."

* * *

The nighttime walk wasn't very far. They had chosen the UNA Hotel Roma because of its proximity to the train station, but also because of how close it was to the chamber location described in the journal. They reached the edge of what should have been the cemetery in no time at all. Much to their surprise, there was no cemetery. There was only the sight of bulldozers, backhoes, and lots of other equipment surrounded by a ten-foot high chain link fence topped with barbed wire.

"Is this what you expected?" Katie asked.

"Not at all," Luke answered. "Now, even if it hasn't been crushed by all those trucks, without the landmarks, we'll never find the chamber."

"We can still try to take a look," Katie replied.

Tommy surveyed the fence. He found a section where rain run-off had eroded a trench beneath the chain link. He bent down, grabbed the bottom edges of the fence and hoisted with all his might. The metal curled under his pressure, creating a small opening. Billy scurried through, Lynn quickly followed. Katie slid under on her back, and Luke was barely able to squeeze through. All four of them stood safely on the other side.

"What about me?" Tommy asked.

"You'll have to stay there," Luke said. "You can help us get out when were done."

"But I want to see the chamber," Tommy protested.

"How are you going to get in?" Katie asked. "You're too big to fit through the opening, and we can't bend it."

Tommy took a long look. In a split second, he made a decision. He backed up and took a running leap at the fence, scaling the barrier in two catlike strides. When he reached the top, he grabbed the pole with his left hand and carefully grabbed the wire, between the barbs, with his right. In a magnificent feat of gymnastic strength, he shifted his body into a handstand, keeping himself balanced upside down on the top of the fence, before vaulting his body over, landing safely on the other side.

Luke and Katie stood open mouthed, stunned by what Tommy had just done.

"Well come on," Tommy said, "we have a chamber to find."

"Did you see that?" Katie asked.

Luke didn't answer. He just stared at his brother in disbelief.

They moved into the darkened construction site, weaving through the shadows, in between the large vehicles. All of the ground looked the same, now that the bulldozers and backhoes had done their work. There were no tombstones and no buildings; nothing to let them know where to start the search.

"This is hopeless," Luke confessed. "Without any landmarks, we'll never find the chamber."

"Are you saying we should give up?" Katie asked.

Luke didn't have a chance to respond. The whole area lit up in a flood of bright light. A voice boomed from the distance, "Chi è lì? Cosa stai facendo qui? Questo posto è off limits." The voice was followed by a second sound, a group of rowdy barking dogs. Both sounds got louder and closer.

"We need to get out of here," Katie said, "now!"

"We'll never make it," Tommy replied, "they're too close and they're blocking the way to the hole under the fence."

"I'll lead them away," Luke said. "Tommy, you take Billy... Katie, you take Lynn. We'll meet at the museum."

"I don't know," Katie said. "We shouldn't split up."

"We don't have any choice," Luke explained. "You need to get Billy and Lynn out of here."

Reluctantly, Katie agreed. Tommy grabbed Billy in his arms. Lynn climbed up onto Katie's back. Together, they hid behind one of the oversized wheels of the backhoe, waiting for their chance to escape.

Luke stepped out into the open. The bright lights shined down on him, the sound of the approaching man and the dogs got louder and louder. He stayed in the open long enough for them to see him. Once he was sure he was spotted, Luke dashed away, drawing their chase. He weaved between vehicles and sprinted as fast as his legs would carry him.

The dogs were quicker than he expected. They were on him in an instant, nipping at his heels and the pack on his back. He dodged left and then dodged right, but it was no use, they tracked his every move. Luke jumped onto the back of a bulldozer and climbed. The dogs jumped too, snagging his pants and dragging him backwards. He fell hard to the ground, three barking German Shepherds around him.

19. Dog Meat

Luke tried to roll away, but the German Shepherds stayed with him, matching him move for move, teeth bared, growling ferociously. They were about to have him for dinner when a booming voice stopped the dogs in their tracks. "Heel," the man said. The dogs immediately backed away from Luke and fell in behind their master.

The man was a mountain unto himself; he carried a steel crowbar in his hand. His thick, scruffy beard covered a pock marked face, denim overalls covered a bulging gut. He took one look at Luke and laughed. "Tu sei ciò che questo polverone è tutto? Sei un pezzo magro di un niente. Cosa stai facendo in un cantiere di notte? Sei venuto a controllare le grandi autocarri ragazzino?"

Luke didn't say a word. He just looked up while his whole body shook with nerves.

The man bent down on one knee to get closer. The three dogs paced behind him. "You no speak Italiano? Do... you... speak... English... little boy?"

Luke didn't know what to make of this man. Was he in trouble? Was he going to go to jail? He didn't know what to do or what to say.

"Aw man, I thought all you kids around here at least knew a little English," the man growled. Then in a very slow drawl he added, "You... can't... be... here... You... have... to... leave."

Without a word, Luke ran from the man and the dogs, and out the front gate of the construction site.

* * *

It took a while, but Luke gathered his composure on the walk to the museum. The others were waiting for him in front when he arrived.

"How did you get away?" Katie asked. "We saw the dogs chasing you."

"You know me," Luke answered. He pointed to the tear in his pants and added, "They almost got me, but I made some nifty moves and got away."

"I can't believe it, I thought you were a goner," Katie said. "First Tommy with the fence and now you with the dogs; you guys are full of surprises."

"It was nothing," Luke responded. "Let's just get our tickets and go inside."

Luke picked up their pre-paid tickets at the admission counter. He handed them out to his brothers and cousins, and together they passed through the large lobby and into the museum.

"The woman at the counter didn't know anything about the Soren Jacobsen exhibit," Luke said, "so we're going to need to find a curator or someone who can help."

"Luke look," Katie called. She found a schematic showing the entire layout of the museum. It was all in Italian, but nothing said "Soren Jacobsen."

Luke tried to ask several people for help, but either they didn't speak English or, if they did, they had no idea who Soren Jacobsen was. Finally, Luke threw up his hands in disgust.

"Maybe we can find it if we split up," Katie offered.

"Fine," Luke replied, "you take Lynn, Tommy you take Billy. We'll meet back here in twenty minutes."

Katie and Lynn moved in one direction, Tommy and Billy moved in another. The museum was so big, it was going to take a while to find anything.

Luke wandered aimlessly until frustration got the better of him. Finally he plopped down on a bench, not sure what to do next.

"Why so glum chum?"

The words startled Luke. When he looked up, he saw the smiling face of a beautiful woman. She wore oversized glasses and a docent's uniform, and her brown hair was cut in a bob.

"You're American," Luke said.

"I am," she replied with a giggle.

"And you know about this museum?" he asked hopefully.

"I do," she answered. "I'm here in Italy studying art history."

"Can you help me?" he asked, excitedly.

"I'll try," she said with a laugh. Luke's growing exuberance amused her.

"I'm trying to find an exhibit, by the Danish inventor, Soren Jacobsen."

"Oh," she responded, her voice changed from her upbeat tone.

Luke's moment of joy quickly faded. "You've never heard of Soren Jacobsen have you?"

"It's not that," she said, her voice still melancholy. "It's just that they moved the exhibit."

"Where?" Luke responded.

"It was given to a museum specifically for Soren Jacobsen's inventions."

"Really," Luke said, unable to contain his excitement.

"Yes... but..." She said the words slowly, afraid of dashing his hopes. "It's a long way away... it's in Greece."

"It is?" Luke replied. "That's great!"

"It is?" she laughed.

"Oh thank you." Luke wrapped his arms around her and gave her a big hug. "Thank you, thank you, thank you!"

*   *   *

When the others returned from their search of the museum, they found Luke sitting on the bench, smiling like the Cheshire cat.

"We searched everywhere, but we didn't find anything," Katie said.

"You won't find anything because they don't have any Soren Jacobsen artifacts here," Luke said, still smiling from ear to ear.

"Then why are you so happy?"

"Because I found out where they are... it's an entire museum dedicated to Soren Jacobsen."

"That's great, where is it?"

"It's in Greece, our very next stop."

*   *   *

It had been a long day with all the travel, the trip to the cemetery and then the museum. Back at the hotel everyone fell asleep rather quickly, everyone except Luke that is. Luke waited for everyone to fall asleep, and then snuck down to the hotel business center.

The computers in the business center offered internet access. Luke used the opportunity to research everything he could about the new museum in Greece. It was late by the time he snuck back into the hotel room, and it seemed like no sooner had his head hit the pillow than the morning alarm went off.

It was a mad scramble getting everyone ready in the morning. Billy and Lynn were not generally cooperative at any time of day, but even less so in the morning. Tommy was a bear to get out of bed even on his best day, and Luke was struggling to gain his composure after a very late night.

Katie was the only one on time, and she was frustrated trying to get everyone in line. "Come on, get moving!" she shouted. But she didn't stop there. She kept on top of all four of them until everyone was packed, dressed and out the door.

It was a short walk to Roma Termini where they boarded the high speed rail to Bari, Italy. There, they picked up a very turbulent ferry ride from Bari to Patra, Greece.

The train and ferry rides were part of their preplanned itinerary and paid for, thanks to Dad's credit card. They had private compartments on each, and vouchers for food. Tommy and Katie took Billy and Lynn to the dining room while Luke researched their itinerary and planned their arrival. He wanted to make the most of every moment, and didn't want to risk getting lost.

When the others returned with the food, Luke was excited to share where they were going next. "When we get there, we're going straight to the museum. I had to make a few changes to our plan, but I think it'll work out."

20. Argentina Once Again

It had been a while since either Uncle Al or Abigail had been to the old church and cemetery, but it still looked the same--run down, weathered and completely overgrown. To Yousef and his men, it was all entirely new and unsettling, like the location of a potential ambush with danger waiting behind every turn.

"There better not be any surprises," Yousef barked. He directed his men to keep a close eye on their captives. "We're watching your every move, don't try anything."

Uncle Al wasn't planning to try anything, not here anyway, not out in the open where a bullet from any one of those guns could bring a quick end to his existence. He led the men through the cemetery to the back end of the lot and through the brush that had regrown since the last time he was here. They came to a collection of headstones, nine in all, arranged to form a perfect square.

"Now what?" Yousef asked, impatiently.

Uncle Al used his hand to direct two of Yousef's men to the tombstones on the eastern corners. "Stand next to them," he said. They first looked at their leader, and, after receiving a nod from him, did as they were told. Uncle Al then crossed to the headstone in the middle on the opposite side. He leaned on top of the stone, using all of his weight to push it down. It shifted several inches. "Now push down on your stones," he directed the men.

The two men pushed down on their headstones. Everyone was stunned to see the tombstone between them shift on its own, and even more surprised to see the entryway that lay behind.

"You," Uncle Al shouted, pointing at another of Yousef's men, "come over here and lean on this!" The man did as he was told. Uncle Al then moved to the opening and, with one hand, pushed the stone aside, revealing a passageway leading deep into the cold earth. Uncle Al turned to Yousef. "There's the entrance," he said. "I did my part, can we leave now?"

"Nice try," Yousef growled. "You first."

Uncle Al signaled to Abigail who got down on her knees and crawled into the tunnel. Uncle Al followed. Yousef and his men approached cautiously.

Before the first of the men could enter, Uncle Al popped his head out. "There's been a cave in," he announced. "We're going to need to do some digging."

"*You're* going to need to do some digging," Yousef answered. "Get to it."

Uncle Al turned his body back into the tunnel and began shoveling mounds of dirt towards the entrance. "Abigail and I are doing all the work. Can your guys at least help move it from here?" Uncle Al asked. Yousef nodded to his men, and immediately they began moving it away. After an hour of intense digging, Uncle Al popped his head out of the tunnel and announced, "I think we have a big enough opening." He then ducked back inside and crawled through.

He didn't get five feet into the tunnel before a hand grabbed his ankle. "Don't get too far ahead," a voice growled.

The tunnel walls, floor, and ceiling were hardened dirt and supported by deteriorating wooden beams. They came upon several points where the ceiling had collapsed. The passage was so small that everyone was forced to slither on their stomachs to get through. For several hundred feet, they crawled until they emerged in an open chamber cut from stone.

Uncle Al placed a lantern on the floor in the center of the chamber, revealing the details of this finely crafted dome, the arc of the ceiling, and five exits--open portals that led to who knew where.

Yousef was the last to enter. He studied the room, the portals, and the strange writing on the walls. He directed one of his men to photograph every detail. He looked around at all of the people in the room: his men and Uncle Al. Realizing that someone was missing, he turned to Uncle Al and shouted, "Where is your friend, the woman?"

Uncle Al looked around, and noticing that Abigail wasn't there, answered, "She must have gone down one of the tunnels."

This angered Yousef. "Is this your plan, to escape in this underground maze? It's not going to work." He directed two of his men, "Seize him and don't let him out of your sight." Two men grabbed Uncle Al on either side. Yousef stepped forward, pressing his face close to Uncle Al. "Tell me, where did she go?"

Uncle Al stuttered, "I...I...I...I'm not sure."

"You better figure it out," Yousef barked.

"She probably went down there," Uncle Al answered, directing his restrained hand toward one of the open passages.

"Then we go after her," Yousef responded.

Uncle Al stepped towards the doorway, a goon on either side of him. The corridor wasn't wide enough for them to pass through side by side. "Do you mind?" he asked. The men let go, and Uncle Al stepped through the door, disappearing into the darkness.

"Stay close to him," Yousef barked.

The men raced into the corridor, shining their flashlights in time to see Uncle Al scurry to the far end of the corridor.

* * *

Outside, at the square of tombstones, Abigail had a different perspective. She watched as Uncle Al turned to Yousef. "There's the entrance, I did my part, can we leave now?"

"Nice try," Yousef growled, "you first."

Abigail looked at Uncle Al and saw the glint in his eye. That was the signal. It was time to put their plan into action. She moved toward the opening behind the tombstone, catching Yousef's eye as she prepared to enter. It was a good thing she still had the scarf on or he might have read the signs on her face.

The tunnel was exactly as she remembered; walls, floor and ceiling cut from hardened earth, supported by wooden beams that were well past their expected life cycle. Abigail scurried through as fast as her little body could take her. The plan was for her to escape while Uncle Al pretended the tunnel had collapsed. She needed to act fast. As soon as she reached the domed chamber, she looked back through the tunnel. She couldn't see anything, but she heard Uncle Al's voice, "There's been a cave in. We're going to need to do some digging."

That was her signal to set to work. She approached the mariner's compass in the center of the floor, and turned the dial, opening each of the door portals.

She knew exactly which doorway to take, she had done this before, but even so, there was a slight hesitation. All the doors looked the same and there was no margin for error. Any misstep could be the difference between life and death.

She wedged her body into the opening, trying not to open the door any more than she had to. Inside, she used her flashlight to guide her to the end of the thin corridor where she found three mariner's compass dials on the wall--one to the left, one to the right and one directly in front of her. She turned the dials exactly as she remembered. Even though she should have been expecting it, the weightlessness of falling down the chute still caught her by surprise. Her body twisted and turned with the bends of the slide. Before she knew it, her body was spinning on a hardened tile floor.

It took a moment to regain her composure, but as quick as she could, she hopped to her feet and crossed the room. She had only the beam from her flashlight to guide the way. The light fell upon a collection of beautiful stained glass windows, each depicting scenes from the Bible. There was Abraham sacrificing Isaac, Noah and the ark, Moses parting the sea, Jonah in the belly of the whale, and Jesus on the cross. She approached the window with Jesus on the cross and used her fingers to caress the smooth glass. It took her a moment, but she found what she was looking for, a small opening in the shape of a cross. She reached up to her neck and withdrew a brown leather cord, on the end of which was the cross, given to her by Uncle Al. She inserted it into the opening, and the entire panel shifted on a hidden hinge, revealing a pathway behind. She slipped through the opening and then removed the cross. The panel closed shut behind her.

21. Fitting the Pieces

It was early morning by the time Mom and Dad caught up with Aunt Janine and her crew in Czestochowa, Poland. They found them at another one of Aunt Janine's many hotels, a beautiful facility with all of the trademarks of a Harmon Enterprise establishment, including an ultra plush décor and an oversized fish tank in the center of the lobby.

Finding them wasn't difficult. The itinerary was like a Bible for Aunt Janine and her crew. They stuck to it like clockwork.

"You're just in time," Janine said to them. "We're heading to the next chamber. So where's your brother and his lovely bride?"

"They went home," Mom replied.

"So they've had enough adventure for one trip?" Janine said.

"You could say that," Mom said.

"And you?" Aunt Janine asked. "Have you had enough?"

"My feelings haven't changed," Mom answered. "I want to know more. I *need* to know why my boys are in the middle of this and what is going to happen to them."

The look on Dad's face made it clear how he felt. He was ready to put this entire business behind them. But he would never leave Mom. Wherever she went, he would follow.

There was a van waiting to take them to their next destination. It was only a short ride. When they got out of the van, they were in front of a small stone cottage. It had an old-fashioned thatched roof and was surrounded by a bramble of thorns and wild flowers. From the outside it looked deserted, but once they were inside, it was obvious that someone lived there. The main room was a kitchen and there was a loft above for sleeping.

"We have to be quick," Janine instructed her crew, "the woman and her daughter will be back in a couple of hours."

"Wait," Mom said, "who lives here?"

"It's not important," Janine replied, "what is important is that this is the entrance to the chamber and we need to be in and out before they get back."

No-Neck and The Walrus moved an old farm table from the center of the room and then slid the rug aside. There was a panel in the wood floor. Kerri used a knife from the kitchen drawer to pry it up. Aunt Janine instructed No-Neck and The Walrus to stand lookout. One by one they descended the ladder to another of Soren Jacobsen's chambers, this one hidden beneath a one room cottage in Czestochowa, Poland.

The ladder brought them down in the center of the room. It was definitely one of Soren Jacobsen's creations, but different from most of the other chambers they had visited. It did not have the trademark domed roof, nor did it have the interesting alcoves. Instead, it was purely functional--a square room with stone walls, and an altar on one side. Behind the altar was an elaborate stained glass window depicting a scene from the Bible. The artwork was phenomenal, Jonah praying to God from the belly of a whale.

Dad moved to get a closer look. He pointed to an image at the edge of the stained glass window of a horizontal line with a vine wrapped around it. "This image is familiar, we've seen it in most, if not all, of the locations. But not always the same... more like a theme and variation."

"What do you mean?" Mom asked.

"Sometimes it's horizontal and sometimes it's on a slant... and the way the edges are, it's like... they're incomplete... like they're cut off from a larger image."

Janine stepped forward, interested in what Dad had to say. "And what about this?" she said, pointing to another image on the wall. It was a crisscross of flags, three of them: one black, one white, and one green. "We've seen this one in other chambers."

"I'm familiar with the image," Dad answered, "but in another context. Here it must mean something different."

"Are you sure it's out of context?" Janine prodded.

"What does it mean?" Mom inquired.

Dad took off his glasses and used the bottom of his shirt to clean the lenses. He put the glasses back on and took a closer look. "It's traditionally associated with the sword of the prophet, but it doesn't make sense here. Soren Jacobsen was clearly a Christian; I don't know why that would be here."

"And Holger Danske," Janine added, "any association there?"

Dad looked at her with a long, meaningful glare. "Surely you can't be serious?"

"I'm just asking questions, but you and I both know it makes sense," Janine said.

"Is this why you brought us here? To develop wild theories?" Dad asked, a look of indignation on his face.

There was an extended silence between them. Mom looked on, unsure of what was happening. "What? What is it? What aren't you saying?"

Dad looked sternly at Janine.

"You can tell her, it's just a *wild* theory after all," Janine said in her mocking tone.

Dad stood silent.

"What is it?" Mom insisted.

He turned to her and spoke very softly, "The image of the three flags, one black, one white and one green, is associated with the sword of the prophet." He paused, contemplating his next words.

Mom had already heard this, and anxiously awaited what would come next. She knew better than to interrupt his train of thought; he was trying to find just the right way to communicate the news. She had seen this before. The more difficult the message, the longer it would take. This one seemed to be taking forever.

"The sword of the prophet is associated with ancient teachings." Again Dad paused.

"At the end of the eighth century, Holger Danske fended off an attack on Denmark, preserving the Christian way of life for the Danish people."

Dad paused again, it seemed that he may have been done, but then Janine cut in, "And King Charlemagne…"

Dad looked at her cross. "And King Charlemagne. He and his men defeated the same attacking forces in what is now northern France, keeping them from entering the Frankish empire."

Mom cut in, "So what does that have to do with us?"

Dad did not respond, but Janine was happy to reply, "Durendal, Joyeuse and Curtana. That's what it has to do with us. All three swords were there for those battles. They were created for that purpose."

Mom was confused, "For what purpose?"

Janine gloated as she said, "To defeat the sword of the prophet."

"But that was hundreds of years ago," Mom said in disbelief.

Dad cut in, "Is this why you brought us on this trip? To convince us that our family is in the middle of a holy war?"

Janine's face lit up. She had been waiting for this; she was not going to let it pass without savoring the moment. "Your family doesn't have to have anything to do with this. I never wanted you involved in the first place. We needed you to open Holger Danske's tomb in Denmark, after that you didn't need to be involved."

"But only a couple of months ago you lured us to France and to Sir Roland's chamber with that fake journal," Mom replied indignantly.

"That was when I thought that King Charlemagne's sword Joyeuse was still hidden."

"Then why are we here? Why do you keep involving us?"

"We have the sword, Durendal, and the Manillo family has the sword, Joyeuse. You are in possession of the last piece of the puzzle."

The realization hit Mom. "You want Curtana?"

"You don't have to have anything more to do with this. You and your family can be safe. You can go home to your comfy little lives and pretend none of this ever happened."

"This is why you agreed to bring us on this trip," Dad said. "It wasn't to help us; it was because we had something that you wanted all along."

Janine did not answer. She just looked at Dad expectantly.

"Why didn't you just lure us away and then steal it?"

Again she did not respond.

Dad thought about the situation. "You can't take it can you? It doesn't belong to you and it won't work for you." He paused, letting it all sink in. "Fine, you can have it, as long as you leave my family out of your plans from now on."

But Mom interrupted, "It's not ours to give. Curtana belongs to Luke, he'll need to make the decision."

Janine laughed, but then realized that Mom wasn't joking. "You can't be serious; he's a twelve year old boy. You can't leave the fate of the world to the decision of a twelve year old boy."

"He's thirteen," Mom corrected, "and he's capable of much more than you give him credit for."

"Then I guess we need to ask Luke," Janine said in her cold and calculated tone.

22. It's All Greek To Me

The museum was a gigantic building. The vaulted ceiling of the lobby echoed their footsteps as Luke and the others crossed the floor to a small crowd gathered at the bottom of a marble staircase. They all looked up to a man in a white lab coat, standing on a platform at the top of the stairs.

"If you're looking for dragons or vampires, or warlocks with wands you'll need to look somewhere else because they don't exist. But if it is magic that you seek then you have come to the right place because magic exists for those who will open their eyes long enough to see it." The man in the white lab coat, *the Professor,* as he called himself, had a flare for the dramatic, a showman focused on capturing the imagination and attention of his audience. He was doing a superb job. The small crowd of people hung on his every word.

"I used to hold fast to the notion that science could explain everything," the Professor continued, "as long as you had all of the facts. But there are some things in life that are beyond our feeble contemplation. This presentation is about some of those things.

"Make no mistake, just because you and I cannot explain these fascinating inventions, does not mean that they are not real, nor does it mean that they are not magic.

"Today we are going to show you a collection of items, designed and created by a wizard by today's standard, but who lived hundreds of years ago. Some of his inventions may seem quite ordinary and others may seem unimportant, but let me assure you magic lies within each and every one of them for those who are prepared to see it.

"Take the journey with us into the life and creations of Soren Jacobsen. You can purchase your tickets at the window. Prepare to be amazed." The Professor took a bow and disappeared through a set of double doors behind him. The sign overhead read "Auditorium."

A woman in a multi-colored vest stepped forward to address the crowd. "Anyone needing tickets, please go to the window to the left; if you already have your tickets, please form a single line over here on the right."

Luke led the others to the ticket window and paid the cashier for five tickets. They got in line and waited to go up the stairs and into the auditorium. The line moved slowly, each person had to pass through a security scanner before they could enter.

"That's a pretty sophisticated security system," Katie marveled. "What do you think they're so worried about?"

"They have the inventions of Soren Jacobsen," Luke replied. "I bet they're priceless."

Katie looked around at the marble tile, vaulted ceilings, and pillars. "This place is pretty incredible; I'm surprised more people don't know about it."

Luke and the others passed through the scanning system and into the auditorium. The inside was a little bit of a letdown compared to the lobby. A collection of mismatched folding chairs, arranged in crooked lines, faced a homemade stage. Old red velvet curtains with golden tassels lined either side of the stage, and crudely developed scene sets filled the background. The walls were covered with weathered paper posters depicting various performances that had once graced this theater.

The hairs on the back of Luke's neck stood on end. His excitement was palpable. He whispered to Katie, "What do you think they're going to show us? The Professor was really excited. I bet it's going to be great."

"Don't get too worked up," Katie responded. "I'm sure all that talk was just Barnum and Bailey type promotion. It's a business, and they're trying to sell tickets."

"How can you think like that? You know there's magic in his creations," Luke balked.

"You know that and I know that," Katie replied, "but if this show was really magic, do you think it would be in a second rate theater in the back streets of Athens?"

"No, I guess not," Luke admitted.

A small crowd had gathered and paid the five euros each to get in, so that said something. A young couple, presumably on their first date, entered and grabbed a seat along the back wall. They seemed more interested in each other than anything that might take place on the stage. A family of five--Mom, Dad, two girls about Tommy's age, and a boy a little older than Billy--was selecting their seats. The girls spotted Tommy and tried their best to get his attention. The mother did all she could to keep the little boy under control. Another family--Mom, grandmother, and a toddler-- took seats right in front. Luke led his brothers and cousins across to the far side of the room, and plopped down in the third row, eyes intent on the five draped tables on the stage.

The Professor waited for everyone to file in. He stood in the middle of the stage, surrounded by the draped tables, each covered by a shabby blanket hiding some special surprise. It was obviously meant to heighten the mystery and intrigue of what was about to be revealed.

Satisfied that everyone was settled, the Professor cleared his throat, the sound was magnified by the microphone attached to his collar. "Testing, testing, can everyone hear me?"

No one responded, but it was clear that everyone could hear the booming voice in the tiny theater.

"Welcome everyone and thank you for joining us for this presentation of 'The Magnificent Magical Creations of Soren Jacobsen.' This collection of artifacts from the great Danish inventor will amaze and astound as he stretches the laws of science to bring you the incredible and the impossible.

"The first item I'm going to share with you is a relatively common item today, but several hundred years ago, when Soren Jacobsen first deployed the physics of this creation, it was way ahead of its time." With a dramatic swoop of his arm, the Professor pulled the blanket from the table at the front of the stage to reveal an intricate contraption. It stood about nine inches wide and five inches tall, and from what could be seen from the auditorium seating, it was a collection of interlocking levers.

Luke nudged Katie and whispered, "It's the nutcracker that Uncle Al told us about."

The Professor called out, "Can anyone tell me what this is?"

The dad from the family of five answered, "It's a nutcracker."

"Ah," the Professor laughed, "you are very observant. When we first received this we also thought it was a nutcracker, but, after several years of intense study, we found out that this magnificent creation, using these levers and fulcrums, can generate over twenty thousand kilograms of pressure per square centimeter, far more power than would ever be needed to crack a nut. We believe this device was designed to destroy enemy weaponry." No sooner had the words come out of the Professor's mouth than he grabbed a sword from the bottom shelf of the table and twirled it above his head in dramatic fashion. As quickly as he spun, he lowered the blade and pointed it towards the audience. "This, dear people, is hardened steel, one of the most durable items created by man." He spun his body and swung the sword, shearing off the corner of a block sitting at the edge of the stage. A few people gasped, and the family in the front row jumped back.

"There's nothing to be afraid of," the Professor laughed. "I just wanted to show you the strength of the steel before I did this." He inserted the blade into the device on the table. He then grabbed the handle of the contraption, and with three fluid motions, he compressed, compressed, compressed, moving the blade further and further into the device with each thrust. Each movement of the blade transformed it more, bending and contorting the hardened steel. By the time he was done, the sword was unrecognizable, a completely different object. He held it up for everyone to see. It looked like a garden hoe. "A harmless garden tool," he laughed, "more suitable for tending your tomatoes than fighting a war."

113

The audience stood and stared. It was obvious the Professor expected more of a response. And finally, when he took a dramatic bow, he was greeted by a smattering of applause.

"Thank you, thank you," he said with another bow. "And now, for our next revelation I will need a volunteer from the audience." As he said this, he slid the cart with the sword crusher to the side and rolled a new cart to the center of the stage. All of the kids had their hands stretched high, trying to get his attention to be called on stage. He took a moment, as if he was surveying a crowd of thousands, before finally calling on one of the girls who had been trying to flirt with Tommy. She bounced up to the stage and stood next to the Professor, first waving to her family, and then staring and smiling at Tommy.

The Professor cleared his throat. "This next invention still baffles us today; we are not sure how it works, but it has proven accurate in over a thousand uses." He turned to his new helper and said, "And young lady, what is your name?"

She giggled bashfully and said, "I'm Diana."

"Well Diana, I'm glad you could join us today. Did you come from far away?"

Again she giggled and, in an English accent responded, "Yes, we're from England." In the audience, her parents clapped loudly as if she had just answered a very difficult question.

The Professor asked her, "I was wondering if you could help me out with this next display?"

"Oh yes," she responded eagerly, quite excited to see what was under the blanket.

"This next invention from Soren Jacobsen has the ability to tell where you have traveled, and, as I've said before, we are unable to explain how it works." He pointed to the cart and said, "Diana would you do me the honor of revealing the next device?"

Diana had been waiting for the word, and quickly grabbed the corner of the covering and yanked it free. Before their eyes stood a beautiful globe of the world, but this globe was different from any that had been seen before.

The Professor explained, "As you will see, this is a globe of the world, however; this is unlike any we've come across before." He took a long pointer from the lower shelf of the table and directed everyone's attention to different points on the globe. "As you can see, this globe has no axis. In fact, it is not touching the base or the frame at any point." He used the pointer to pass completely around the globe, showing that it hovered in the center of the base without contact. "Diana, will you please show everyone that the globe is not connected to anything?" He handed her a yellow ring from the table.

Diana used the ring to pass around the globe, clumsily bumping against it. The globe shifted under the contact, but returned to its rightful place in a matter of seconds.

"Now this alone might seem extraordinary, but the hovering properties could be explained by magnetic forces present in both the globe and the frame. No, this creation, by the famed Soren Jacobsen, is so much more."

He turned back to his lovely assistant and said, "Diana do you know how you got here today?"

"We took a cab from the hotel," she responded, and again her parents applauded.

"Yes, yes," the Professor replied, "but I was talking in a grander scale. Do you know how you traveled here from England?"

Diana was stumped by the question. She looked to her parents in the audience for help. Finally she responded, "By Plane?"

The Professor laughed and then said, "Perhaps your father would come up to help you with this." The Professor motioned to Diana's father who readily rose from his seat and joined his daughter on the stage.

"Okay Dad," the Professor said, "I'd like you to keep an eye on the globe while Diana touches it." He bent down to Diana and said, "Are you ready little lady?"

Diana nodded excitedly. She stepped forward and smiled broadly at her father.

The Professor instructed her, "I want you to place your finger on the globe where you live."

Diana looked at the globe, and with her father's assistance, found her hometown, London, England. She rested the tip of her finger on London and no sooner had she touched it than the globe began to move.

"Dad," the Professor said, "can you tell us what's happening?"

Dad's face lit up and his eyes just about popped out of his head. "It moved, first to Paris, then Venice and Rome and now..." he paused as the globe continued to move, "and now Athens."

Once again the audience paused, not sure how to respond. But then the Dad on the stage stepped back and began to clap loudly. He was so impressed by the trick, he started to cheer, and as he did, the rest of the crowd followed suit. The Professor was thrilled at the reaction and took several deep bows before sending Diana and her father back to their seats.

"That is just the tip of the iceberg when it comes to the fascination of Soren Jacobsen and his inventions," the Professor exclaimed. "So who would like to see another amazing feat?"

The audience erupted. The Professor was thrilled. He stepped around the stage, slid the table with the globe off to the side and then pulled another covered table from the back of the stage. He dramatically spun it in circles before bringing it to rest front and center. "Before I unveil this next device, I would like to give you a little background on this creation."

"There is much about Soren Jacobsen that we do not know, like when and where he was born, and his family life. And while he was known to travel extensively, we are still uncertain of all the places he visited and what he did when he went abroad. But what we do know is that he was highly renowned and was commissioned by famous kings and queens to create very special items.

"This next creation is very special indeed. Before I reveal this item, I was wondering if there was someone in our audience who might want to help?"

Just like before, a group of hands shot into the air. Little heads bobbed up and down, trying to get the Professor's attention. He looked over the bright shiny faces, considering each one carefully. Finally, he lifted his arm and pointed at a young boy in the third row. "You," he said, "can you come join me on the stage and help me with this?"

117

A bunch of tiny heads whipped around and stared as Billy moved from his seat and toward the stage. He scrambled up the steps and joined the Professor next to the table at the front of the stage.

"Well young man," the Professor said, "what's your name?"

"Billy."

"Well Billy, are you a fan of Soren Jacobsen?"

"Uh huh."

"You are?" the Professor laughed. "You must have been really paying attention. Do you know what's under this cover?"

"Uh uh."

The Professor got down to Billy's level. "Would you like to find out?"

"Yeah," Billy responded, and before the Professor could say anything else, Billy reached around him, grabbed a corner of the blanket and yanked the cover off of the table to reveal a beautiful golden crossbow emblazoned with red rubies. Many "oohs" and "ahs" emitted from the crowd.

The Professor was stunned by Billy's reaction. He missed the opportunity to revel in the unveiling, but quickly gathered his composure. He stepped in front of the table and addressed the crowd, "And here we have another of Soren Jacobsen's inventions: a crossbow, commissioned by the King of the Francish Empire.

"As the story goes, Soren Jacobsen never delivered this item to the King, feeling it was too special for even the King to have. There is also a legend that this crossbow has

118

special properties. However, no matter how many tests we have performed on it, we have yet to discover anything new."

As the Professor spoke to the group, Billy climbed up on the table and took the crossbow into his hands. When he did, the red rubies lit up and the handle of the crossbow magically began to glow.

23. Hot on the Trail

The crowd stared in disbelief. Billy held the crossbow, his smile brighter than any of the glowing rubies. The Professor was so shocked, he was unable to say or do anything.

The hairs on the back of Luke's neck stood on edge. It wasn't the events on the stage that had him unnerved. It was something else. He wasn't sure what it was at first, but a quick glance over his shoulder and he knew in an instant.

Even in a black suit and fedora hat, Luke would know The Walrus anywhere. The man with the beady eyes and bushy moustache tried to look away, but it was too late. Luke now knew why his senses were tingling.

"We've got company," he announced. His voice was barely an audible whisper.

"Where? Who?" Katie asked, whipping her head around.

"Don't look," Luke tried to say, but he was too late.

"The Walrus!" Katie exclaimed. "And if he's here then..."

"No-Neck," Tommy announced, pointing in the opposite direction at the oversized man with the square head and the gruesome tattoo on the overgrown muscles where his neck should have been.

From opposite directions the two men converged on the youngsters, blocking off all angles of escape.

"Katie, grab Lynn. I'll get Billy. Tommy, lead us out of here." By now they were familiar with quick getaways;

they kept all of their worldly belongings in their backpacks which had become a permanent addition to their attire.

Tommy stormed straight at The Walrus. The man made the mistake of trying to cut him off and Tommy laid into him with a front kick to the groin. Then it was a quick jaunt out the doors and down the stairs, two at a time.

Luke rushed the stage, hoisted Billy into his arms and raced to catch Tommy. Katie struggled to lift her sister, but did all she could to keep up. Luke, with Billy in his arms, vaulted out the door and slid down the banister. Katie did the same with Lynn. They reached the bottom of the steps and headed for the front doors.

"Stop them," The Walrus yelled from the top of the steps, "they've stolen a priceless artifact."

A guard near the doors moved to block the exit. Tommy approached, faked to the left and bolted through the door to the right. When the guard spun to reach for Tommy, Katie and Luke, with the little ones on their backs, slipped through the left door and out onto the sidewalk. Together the five of them bolted across the main avenue, down a side street and across town as fast as they could. They ran and ran until their lungs couldn't take in air fast enough. Finally they came to rest, out of view, in an alley several blocks away.

It wasn't true, they hadn't taken anything, but who would believe them? And besides, they couldn't risk being stopped and questioned, five kids traveling all alone so far from home.

The good news was they had escaped, and as far as they could tell, there was no one following them. But there was bad news as well. Aunt Janine's crew had predicted

121

where they would turn up and now they were wanted by the police. Their whole pre-planned trip was compromised.

"The credit card trail," Katie surmised. "They must have realized we were paying with your Dad's credit card and put a trace on it."

"So that's how they knew we were in Greece?" Luke asked.

"I guess," Katie replied.

"So how did they know we would show up at the museum?" Luke pondered.

"They could have contacted the travel agent and gotten our whole schedule," Katie said. "Once they knew we were in Greece, it'd be easy to figure out where we were going."

Luke thought about it. "But then that means…"

"You got it," Katie said, "we can't go to any of our scheduled hotels and we can't use any of our prepaid tickets."

"But how will we get around? Where are we going to stay?"

Katie stuttered, "I-I-I-I don't know…."

"How much cash do we have?" Luke asked.

Katie held out her money. She had about 150 euros. Tommy turned out his pockets. He had eighty.

"Every little bit counts," Katie countered. "How much do you have?" she asked Luke.

"Almost 200 euros," Luke replied, "but together it's not enough for the five of us."

They looked down at Billy and Lynn who were splashing in a puddle.

"Look on the bright side, it could be worse," Katie reasoned.

"I don't know. We don't know where our parents are, we have no tickets, no place to stay and not much money. It can't get much worse."

And then it started to rain.

24. Better Times

If you've ever wondered, sleeping in an alley on a rainy summer night is no fun at all. Luke and the others found that out first hand. In some ways they were lucky, they found an alley to sleep in. It didn't offer any of the conveniences of home, but it gave them a safe hiding place when they needed it. There was nowhere else they could go. After the events at the museum the police were now hunting them and their pre-planned itinerary was useless. All those warm beds and hot showers would have felt so great right about now.

Despite the dire circumstances, Billy and Lynn endured pretty well. That probably had a lot to do with the fact that they were sheltered behind a dumpster while Luke, Tommy and Katie took turns standing guard. The older kids got no sleep at all as they fought the rain and the constant thought of someone creeping up on them.

Never had a sight been more welcome than when the sun rose that morning. It looked so beautiful. The clouds parted, and warm rays shone down on their drenched clothes and withered bodies. For the first time in the past twelve hours, there was belief that life could be good again.

"What should we do now?" Katie asked. She shook the water out of her hair and stretched her arms and back.

"We have a little money left, I think we should get some food," Luke said.

Everyone perked up at the thought of something to eat. With yesterday's mad scramble chase and the search for a place to sleep, along with the horrible conditions through the night, a bite to eat sounded great. Not to mention, every stomach was bellowing a chorus of growls that sounded like the dog pound just before dinner.

There was a market not too far away, complete with the aromatic smells of fresh baked bread, and the promise of a healthy meal. All of their mouths began to water. They walked through the door and a plump old man, dressed in white with a broom in his hand, met them at the entrance.

"Out...out... out," he said. His words were Greek but the volume of his shout and the swipe of his broom made it quite clear to the kids what he was saying.

"What's the matter?" Luke asked, but before he could get an answer, they were forced out the door by the swinging broom. They found themselves out on the sidewalk in front of the store.

The man shouted again. It was clear they were not welcome in his store.

All five of them huddled together. They were bewildered by what just happened. Luke took a look at their reflection in the store window and realized why they were greeted so rudely.

They were a motley crew to say the least. Their clothes were filthy, their hair was wet and disheveled, and one whiff made it obvious they had spent the night in a dumpster. A drowned rat would have been welcomed more warmly.

"We have money!" Tommy exclaimed.

"But we look like street rats," Luke replied. "We need to think."

Katie pulled the group to the side of the building. "I have a plan," she said. She opened her backpack and withdrew a shirt. It wasn't clean, but certainly looked better than the clothes she was wearing. Luke and Tommy turned their backs and provided cover as Katie made a quick change. She pulled a band from around her wrist, and like she had done thousand times before, pulled her long brown hair back into a tight ponytail, securing it with the band. A few splashes of puddle water on her face and she actually looked presentable. "Stay here with Billy and Lynn," she said. "I'll be back in a jiff."

Katie bounded around the corner with money in her hand, and approached the front of the store. With an entirely different demeanor, she strutted through the doors and past the old man with the broom. He gave her the once over, but didn't stop her. She checked out the fresh baked bread and fresh fruit. After filling a basket with a variety of items, she approached the elderly woman behind the counter.

"Good day," Katie greeted the woman. Her words were flavored with a thick British accent.

"Kalimera," the woman responded, and then in broken English added, "How are you today?"

"Simply dreadful, if you really want to know," Katie said. She offered a glowing smile that did not match her words. "If I told you what I've been through, you wouldn't believe me."

The woman raised her eyes at Katie's words. And, as if on cue, curiosity got the better of her. "What is to be the problem?"

If possible, Katie's glow got even brighter. She recited her story as if she had rehearsed it a thousand times before.

* * *

Outside, in the alley, Luke and Tommy played keep away with a ratty old tennis ball they found in the gutter. Billy and Lynn chased back and forth, back and forth, trying to get the ball. They laughed and giggled until all at once, frustration got the better of them, and they both began to cry.

"Just give it to them," Luke said.

"But we're having fun," Tommy protested.

The cries from the little ones got louder, and soon the sound was echoing throughout the alleyway. "Just let them have it or they'll only get worse."

Reluctantly, Tommy kicked the ball to Billy, and the crying ceased. Billy scooped up the ball and gave it to Lynn, and the two of them shared a secret discussion.

Tommy walked to the front edge of the alley where Luke was peaking around the corner, towards the front of the market. Katie was still inside. "So what do you think she's getting us?" Tommy asked.

"I don't know, but they had pastries and donuts and all sorts of good stuff."

"I'm so hungry I could eat vegetables," Tommy replied. He rubbed his growling stomach.

Luke laughed. "Do you think she'll get us some chocolate? I could really go for some chocolate... and peanut butter."

Tommy didn't have a chance to respond before they saw Katie come out of the market, smiling from ear to ear, a packed satchel in her arms.

"What did you get?" Luke and Tommy asked simultaneously.

Katie was beaming. "I got more than just food."

She set the satchel down and Tommy pulled at the bag. "Bread," he said excitedly. "I've never been so excited for bread before." He tore the fresh loaf into pieces and handed some to the others. "And cheese," he added, taking a bite from the chunk and passing it on. Nothing was said for the next several minutes. Five hungry mouths chewed on the most delicious bread and cheese any of them had ever tasted.

"So what else did you get?" Luke asked, food crumbles falling from his mouth.

"I picked up some fruit and some vegetables," Katie replied. She finished chewing and added, "And I also got us a place to get cleaned up."

"What!?!" Luke almost spit the bread out of his shocked mouth.

Katie's smile grew. "I told the couple who owns the market our story and they offered us their back room. There's a bathroom… with a shower."

"You told them we're on the run?" Luke asked incredulously.

"Well… I may have left some details out, and embellished some others, but let's just say when they heard we got separated from our parents and didn't have any place to stay, they were more than happy to help."

The excitement bubbled throughout the group as they continued to chow down.

"Can we wash our clothes?" Luke asked. "Tommy stinks."

"Yep," Katie said with a laugh, "and we can even sleep there if we want to."

Luke was stunned. "So what exactly did you tell them?"

25. Remote Updates

Aunt Janine's private jet landed at a small airport just outside of Moscow. A driver and his limo were waiting to take Aunt Janine, Mom, Dad and Kerri to their next destination.

"Our group has gotten a lot smaller," Dad joked as he handed his bags to the driver and hopped into the back of the limo.

"Yes," Aunt Janine agreed succinctly.

Dad continued, "I wasn't sure you would continue with this tour now that we know your true motive."

"I told you before," Aunt Janine responded, "It's important for you to learn about this. Once you understand everything I'm sure you'll do the right thing."

Mom interjected, "We already told you, the decision belongs to Luke."

"Of course," Aunt Janine replied. "That's why I sent Elliott and David to collect the children. We'll explain everything when they get here and he'll do the right thing."

Mom was shocked. "You sent your men all the way back to the US?"

Aunt Janine looked at Mom with wide eyes. "You really think your children are at home?" She laughed. "You naïvete would be adorable if it wasn't such an important matter."

"They're not at home," Mom retorted, "they're safe at a camp."

"You don't know your children as well as you think. They never went to that camp, they've been following the journal just like we have."

"We dropped them off ourselves..." Mom started to say, but the words choked in her mouth. She looked to Dad for input. "They are at camp right? You said they'd be safe there." Was it possible? Could the boys have made it to Europe? She wanted to believe they were safe at home but the confidence in Aunt Janine's words gave her doubt.

Aunt Janine looked at her with a condescending glare that resembled pity. "I see all of your *parenting* experience has really paid off." She was about to make another comment when the ringing of her cell phone interrupted.

"Tell me you have good news," she said into the phone. She listened for a moment and then added, "That's most unfortunate. Do you know where they are now? Are you able to track them?" Again she listened before adding, "Remind me again why I pay you? Find them or else."

She hung up the phone abruptly and turned to Mom. "Your children are in Greece, Athens to be specific. But they gave my men the slip and now they're gone."

"Athens?" Mom questioned.

"Yes," Aunt Janine said with a laugh, "Try to keep up. They used your credit card to book a trip across Europe and Asia. All without you knowing."

Mom wasn't sure what was more unnerving, that her boys were travelling all over Europe alone or that Aunt Janine knew more about them than she did. She was about to say something when Aunt Janine's phone rang again.

131

"Tell me you have better news than those numbskulls I sent after the children." After a momentary pause she said, "Stop blubbering Abby, I can't understand a word you're saying."

She listened intently for several moments and then replied, "I see." Her face turned white and her tone went solemn. "Get yourself back to company headquarters, I'll meet you there by week's end."

Aunt Janine hung up the phone and sat in silence, her face blank, the look of condescension gone.

"Is everything okay?" Mom asked.

Aunt Janine did not answer. Instead she lowered the divider leading to the driver and asked, "How long until we get to the cemetery?"

26. Travelling Band

It wasn't the most comfortable situation, but sleeping in a store room is way better than sleeping outside next to a dumpster. And being able to wash away all the filth and grime of the last couple of days was a heavenly experience, even for kids who usually complain every time they are asked to take a shower. By the time they said goodbye to the couple that owned the market, Luke and the others felt like completely different people.

"So how are we going to get to Poland?" Katie asked.

"That's our next destination isn't it?" Tommy added.

Luke was thrilled. After the change in circumstance, he thought for sure they were going to give up, but here they were, ready to move on. He smiled as he thought about the surprise he had for them. "I have these," he said, showing them a packet in his hand.

"What is it?" Katie asked.

"Bus tickets," Luke replied, "from Athens to Czestochowa, Poland." His smile grew even wider.

"But how?" Tommy said. "I thought we couldn't use anything from our travel plan."

"These weren't part of our original plan," Luke replied. "I bought them when we changed plans to go to the museum."

Katie shook her head. "But if you used the credit card, they'll still be able to track it."

"That's the thing," Luke said, "I billed it to our room. It won't show up on the credit card; it will only show up on the hotel bill."

"But they could still see it," Katie offered.

"They could if they got into the hotel records, but I think it's worth the risk... besides, how else would we get there; it's 2300 kilometers."

"Do they serve food on the bus?" Tommy asked. "I'm hungry."

Katie laughed. "When aren't you hungry?"

Luke started to walk. "We'll grab something before we get on the bus. Come on, we've got to get moving if we're going to get there on time."

The walk across town wouldn't have been too bad if they didn't have Billy and Lynn with them. But any walk with a couple of three year olds is its own adventure as well as a test of one's patience. Either their legs were too tired, or they wanted to stop to play, or they wanted to eat, or they basically wanted to do anything but what they were told to do.

By the time they reached the bus station, people were already boarding. Luke and Katie rushed across the parking lot with Billy and Lynn in their arms. Tommy made a quick dash to a nearby market to buy some food.

Tommy made it back just in time, his backpack over his shoulder, a bag of food in one hand, a strange wooden object in the other hand, and a bus ticket in his mouth. The bus driver took the ticket, and Tommy rushed to the back of the bus to meet up with Luke and the others.

"What is that?" Katie asked.

"It's breakfast," Tommy replied. He handed the bag to Katie. "I got olive bread, cheese, yogurt, hard boiled eggs and cereal. They didn't have any of the cereals we usually eat."

"I meant *that*," Katie said, pointing to the strange wooden object in Tommy's hand.

Tommy held it up for her to see. It was a little larger than his hand. and it had a solid wood bar with a button on one end and two sharpened prongs jetting out of the handle. "Oh, this?" Tommy said with a devilish grin. "This is a kubotan. It's cool isn't it? I couldn't pass it up; it was only twenty euros."

"What does it do?" Katie asked.

"It's a weapon," Tommy replied, his grin even wider. "You hold it like this." He placed the bar in his hand with the prongs sticking out between his fingers. "And you either hit with it like this," he said, showing a thrust with his fist. "Or you use the butt end to hit one of the pressure points," he added, demonstrating in slow motion.

"Did you really need that?" Luke asked. "You know we need all the money we can get."

"You never know when something like this can come in handy," Tommy replied. He practiced several moves with his new toy.

The bus pulled out of the station and they were on their way. For the first thirty minutes they were all occupied eating their breakfast. At home, Mom probably never could have gotten them to eat olive bread, or non-sugar cereal for that matter, but go without a steady supply of food for a while, and they were willing to eat just about anything.

It was over six hours of driving before the bus finally came to its first pit stop. In that six hours, Billy and Lynn visited the bus' bathroom seven times, got yelled at by the bus driver four times, spilled three drinks, and started one fight between two old ladies over whose wig looked more natural. By the time the bus pulled into the station in Macedonia, everyone was ready to get off and away from the "American Terrors" as they had come to be known.

* * *

After the break in Macedonia, Luke could feel the stares of disapproval as they boarded the bus. There were new people among the passengers, travelers who had just boarded, but based on the look on their faces, the stories of the "American Terrors" had circulated. Luke wondered how they were going to be able to keep Billy and Lynn in line for this next leg of the trip.

They grabbed seats at the back of the bus, as far away from the crowd as they could get. Not surprising, no one chose to sit anywhere near them. This gave them a little bit of room for Billy and Lynn to play, and also gave them access to the bathroom without disrupting the other passengers.

Luke thought back to other trips he had taken, and the preparations Mom had made in advance of their departure. Mom always packed a separate bag to "occupy" the kids. Now he knew why. In their quick effort to pack for this trip, they did a very good job of securing the essentials, but they never thought about keeping Billy and Lynn entertained.

Luke thought about Mom and Dad, where they were right now, and why they shipped them off to a military camp for the summer. He was both angered and confused. Part of him was angry for being dismissed and shuttled off to camp and, if you could believe it, part of him missed having them around.

He tried to get his mind off his parents. He checked out the others and wondered if they were feeling the same way. Katie was studying a map, Tommy was reading and Billy and Lynn were talking and looking out the window. Why weren't they as bothered as he was? How could they be so relaxed when he was so anxious? He decided it was a good time to catch up on his rest so he laid back in his chair and before he knew it he was fast asleep.

* * *

The bus hit a bump in the road and jolted Luke from his slumber. He didn't know how long he had been out but the environment had completely changed. He was alone at the back of the bus.

Luke got out of his seat and moved forward. Billy was a couple of rows ahead, watching two older men who were deep in conversation. Luke moved forward, ready to apologize for his younger brother, but then he heard their conversation.

"I get the worst rash," one of the men said.

"I know what you mean," the other man replied, "it's terrible."

Billy cut in, "Sometimes my butt itches."

137

The men looked at him and then at one another. Luke's face grew red with embarrassment, but before he had a chance to intervene, the two men answered, "Yeah, that happens to us as well." One of the men tussled Billy's hair.

Billy looked at the pair and said, "Do you ever smell your poop? Mine stinks."

Now Luke was really embarrassed, but the men didn't shoosh Billy away, instead, they burst out laughing. "I'll say," one of the men said, "the food on this trip is wreaking havoc on my insides."

Luke wasn't sure what to do. The men weren't upset with Billy; they seemed to be enjoying his company. He decided to move forward and see what everyone else was up to. He found Lynn a little further ahead; she was dancing in the aisle in the center of a group of women. "Oh those poor women," Luke thought to himself. Lynn finished a tight spin in the confined space, and then bowed. Much to Luke's surprise, the women all responded with a wonderful round of applause, cheering and urging her on.

Luke walked by. What was going on? Billy and Lynn weren't annoying anyone; they seemed to be the life of the party.

At the front of the bus, Katie was telling a story to a group of interested travelers. She was wildly animated, acting out a scene and showing off with various voices and inflections. She said something that Luke couldn't quite make out, but the entire group erupted in laughter. The ruckus didn't have a chance to die down before Tommy stepped up and started a sing-a-long. The song wasn't even in English. Luke didn't know the language, nor did he know the words, but everyone else did, and soon the whole bus was joining in.

Luke sat down in an empty seat. He felt like he was watching an alternate universe or a different dimension. Was this really his brothers and cousins? Did something happen when he was asleep? He turned and looked at the scenery passing by, trying to make sense of the whole situation.

27. Freedom on the Trail

Budapest was the last major stop on the bus trip to Poland. It was a three-hour layover, just enough time to see some sights and stretch their legs. Luke thought it would be best if everyone went for a walk and got some energy out before the final leg.

Luke pulled Tommy and Katie off to the side. "I'll watch Billy and Lynn," he offered, "you guys can go check out the sights."

Tommy didn't want to give him a chance to change his mind, so he took off. Katie looked at him like he had two heads. "Are you sure you'll be okay with the two of them?"

"I'll be fine," Luke assured her. "Go, have some fun."

"Okay," she answered reluctantly.

Luke waited for both Katie and Tommy to be out of sight before he turned to Billy and Lynn. He pulled two hats from his backpack, one red and one yellow. He placed the red hat on Billy's head and the yellow one on Lynn's. Then he pulled some money from his pocket. "Here's some money, you guys go off and have fun, you need to be back here in three hours. Okay?"

Billy looked at Lynn and they exchanged a confused glance. Was he really doing this? They always wanted their freedom, and it seemed like now they were getting it. Together they nodded their heads and started off.

Luke watched them go and thought back to different experiences when Dad would do the same thing with him. No, he didn't just set Luke wild in a foreign city and wait for him to come back. He gave Luke the impression that he was on his own and all the while he followed at a distance, keeping an eye on his son and making sure all was okay.

It was a learning experience that Luke never forgot. He felt the uncertain joy of being on his own, the freedom, the maturity, the responsibility. At times it was scary, and other times liberating, but it forced him to grow, to become more independent and self-sufficient.

What he also didn't know back then, but he did know now, was that Dad was never far behind, observing his son and how he would respond to certain situations, ready to step in if he was really needed.

Luke allowed Billy and Lynn to get about twenty feet ahead and then he followed, weaving in and out of the crowd, being sure that he wasn't seen, but always able to keep an eye on his brother and cousin, or at least their brightly colored hats. In the beginning they stopped every five or ten feet and turned back to look, expecting to see that they were being followed, that they were being watched. But after a while they became accustomed to the freedom, and set off on their own, no longer aware of any constraints.

They walked into a street market and moved between the vendor stalls, checking out the items for sale. Lynn found a handmade doll, fished some money out of her pocket, and paid the woman behind the table. She moved away with her doll and the woman had to chase her down to give her her change. Billy found a cart of toys and bought a small pull train. He paid his money and moved on. Again, the vendor had to chase him down to give him his change.

All the while Luke watched from a distance. He was proud of Billy and Lynn for being able to handle themselves in a foreign city, and he was proud of himself for giving them a little bit of freedom. Letting go of the reigns wasn't easy, but he understood how important it was to let people do their own thing, even if they might make mistakes. He also had a deeper appreciation for Mom and Dad and all of the things they did for him. In that moment he missed them more than he ever had missed anyone before.

Then things changed.

Whenever Dad would let Luke wander off on his own it was just him. It wasn't two kids that Dad had to follow. Billy and Lynn reached a point in the market with shiny jewelry in one direction and colorful fruits in another. Lynn headed for the sparkles and Billy headed for the food.

At first, Luke watched both of them from a distance. To the right, Lynn began pulling necklaces off of a rack, trying to get a closer look. To the left, Billy approached a stack of oranges on a cart and grabbed at the only ones he could reach. In an instant, there was complete chaos. The woman at the jewelry stand was frustrated, screaming at Lynn for messing up her display. The man at the fruit cart started to yell when all of the oranges tumbled off the cart and into the street.

Luke wasn't sure what to do, he couldn't go both ways at once, but they both needed his help. He started toward Lynn but then decided to grab Billy first. In his moment of indecision he lost sight of both of them and they were gone. Panic set in. He raced around, looking for any sign of his cousin or his brother. Where could they have gone? Worst case scenarios surged through his mind.

Then he caught sight of Billy's red hat, scurrying away from the market and toward the river. Luke set off at a harried pace. He was gaining, but Billy was moving fast. When he got closer, he realized that Lynn and her yellow hat were running alongside of Billy. They were together, which was good, but they were headed towards the river and showed no signs of stopping.

The youngsters reached the edge of the river. Luke thought it was his opportunity to catch up, but where there should have been only water, a makeshift pier appeared: a collection of boats, tied together, floating on the water. Billy and Lynn stumbled across the pontoon bridge. Luke reached the edge of the water and called out, "Billy... Lynn... stop!!!"

Together, the two of them looked back. In the process, Billy fell and Lynn tripped over him. They landed hard, and the force of their weight snapped the tether. Luke raced out onto the bridge, but he was too late. The boat that Billy and Lynn were on bobbed violently and split apart from the rest of the pontoon. By the time Luke got there, the boat moved away from the rest of the bridge and began to float downstream.

28. Rushing Rapids

"Stop!" he yelled, but there was no way for Billy and Lynn to stop or even slow the boat down. What could he do?

He tried to shout again, but the roar of an approaching engine drowned out his voice. Luke looked to his right and saw a motorboat steaming towards him. Katie was behind the wheel, waving as she pulled up next to the bridge.

"Billy and Lynn, they're in that boat," Luke said, pointing to the disappearing image downstream. "We need to save them."

"Get in!" Katie shouted.

Luke hopped in the boat. Katie veered away from the bridge, and after Billy and Lynn. The boat was fast and closed the distance quickly.

"Do you see that?" Luke called over the buzz of the engine.

The look of terror on Katie's face made it clear that she saw what Luke saw. A waterfall and raging rapids lay ahead, and Billy and Lynn were headed straight towards it. Katie urged the boat forward. Could they get there fast enough? They gained quickly, but as they approached, the raging waters pushed Billy and Lynn even faster.

Luke leaned over the side of the boat. "Get me close!" he shouted. Katie moved the boat closer, but the cresting water from the surging boat pushed Billy and Lynn even further away. Luke wedged his body between the railing and the side of the speedboat. He extended his entire body over the edge. "Closer!" he yelled again.

144

The waterfall was too close now. There was no way they could stop Billy and Lynn from going over the edge. Katie had a split second to make a decision. If she didn't turn the boat around, they too would be propelled over the waterfall. She pressed the throttle to the max.

Luke stretched out. He was almost close enough to reach his brother and cousin when he felt the boat go airborne. He reached as far as he could, struggling to see through the splashing water. He grabbed with each hand, catching Billy and Lynn by the backs of their shirts and yanking them away just as their pontoon turned over, crashed, and disappeared beneath the turning waters.

The relief was short lived. The speedboat launched over the edge of the waterfall. Luke pulled Billy into his left arm and Lynn in his right, holding them tight. The speed of the boat sent them airborne. He grinned as they floated harmlessly over the raging part of the rapids, but then gasped as the full force of the boat struck hard against the surface of the water, knocking the air out of his lungs and tilting him overboard, Billy and Lynn still in his arms.

The water engulfed them; Luke's body thrashed in the wake. He held Billy and Lynn close and kicked hard with his feet, trying to bring them back to the surface as quickly as possible. He held his breath as long as he could and prayed that neither Billy nor Lynn would take in any water. When they breached the surface, they all gasped for breath, their bodies still moving downstream. By the time they realized where they were, Katie was next to them, using the boat to guide them towards the bank.

On the side of the river they collapsed, exhausted and unable to comprehend everything that had just happened. Luke sucked in the air, refilling his lungs. Katie jumped from the boat and grabbed the little ones into a bear hug. Billy and Lynn started to laugh. Perhaps this was their idea of fun. It may have been the surge of adrenalin or maybe it was the overwhelming stress followed by extreme relief, but Katie and Luke started laughing as well.

It took them a while to collect themselves, but once they did, they left the boat on the river, walked up the bank to a nearby road and managed to find a cab to take them back to the main square.

Tommy was waiting for them when they got back. "There you guys are, I was worried about you," he said excitedly. "I had such an awesome time. I got to see Kossuth Lajos Square, the Kossuth Memorial and the Memorial of the 1956 Revolution. I visited the Hungarian Parliament Building and even went to a museum... by my choice if you can believe that."

Neither Luke nor Katie had the strength to tell their story.

"We better hurry up if we're going to make our bus," Tommy told them. "So what did you guys do... and why are you so wet?"

* * *

It was good to be back on the bus. It may not have been the safest place in the world, but it did provide a sense of security. Billy and Lynn obviously felt secure because as soon

146

as the bus got on the highway, they were asleep in their seats. Katie and Tommy didn't last much longer, and soon Luke was alone with his thoughts once again.

There was nothing to see inside the darkened bus cabin. A few people had reading lights on, but otherwise everyone was drifting off. The only thing Luke could see outside were the streaming headlights of cars passing on the other side of the highway. He decided to occupy his mind with his research and the planning for the next stage of their journey.

The journal pages provided so much information. Luke couldn't get enough of them. Despite the fact that he had read the text many times before, he could not remember the details of the section on Poland and the chamber in Czestochowa. This chamber held particular interest for Luke. This is where Uncle Al found the ball maze, the same ball maze given to him for his birthday, and the magical object that responded to him and him alone. Luke was certain he would find a special connection with Czestochowa and this chamber.

He flipped through the pages, searching for the section on Poland. It was missing. The text went straight from the pages on Greece to the section detailing the cemetery in Russia. Luke went back and forth between the pages, he checked every page to see if somehow they had been placed out of order, but they were nowhere to be found. The journal, that up until now had been the perfect treasure map, was now useless.

Did someone take the pages? Was it Katie? Was it Tommy? Did they not want to find the chamber that held the clues to Luke's involvement in the journey? No, he was being paranoid. But what happened to the pages and what would they do without them?

An overwhelming sense of despair took over. They wouldn't know where to go once they got to Czestochowa, let alone how to get into the chamber even if they were able to find it. Luke was beside himself with angst. How could this be? The one place that was supposed to show him his true connection to the Soren Jacobsen mystery was going to remain just out of reach. There was no way to find it without the journal leading the way.

Luke pondered his options. Perhaps there was another way. They could check out the oldest cemeteries, they could visit the churches and museums in the area. They might even stumble upon something that would help. It was a long shot, but what else could they do? What other choice did they have?

29. Do You Believe in Magic

A collection of brochures at the bus station in Czestochowa gave Luke some clues as to where they should go next. He spied a flyer for a museum in Wrzosowiak. The name sounded familiar, so he decided it was the best place to start.

This museum was not like any museum they had ever been in before. It had the ancient artifacts displayed in glass top display cases, but the confines were tight and there was barely enough room to move. In the past, all the museums that Luke and the others had been to were gigantic buildings with vaulted ceilings and fabulous displays. This was nothing more than an old house with a sign out front.

When they opened the door, a bell rang. An older woman, stern looking with blonde hair done up in a tall beehive, approached. She wore a long red velvet dress and a thick layer of makeup--so thick it was impossible to see her actual skin. Elaborate rings covered every finger, and a gold medallion hung around her neck. The symbol on the medallion was a triangle with a circle around it, and three snakes winding in and out of the curved and straight pieces. Luke thought he had seen the symbol before, but wasn't sure where.

The woman eyed the kids suspiciously. Perhaps she was wary of the damage that Billy and Lynn could cause in her museum filled with delicate objects, and if this was the reason for her behavior, then she had good reason for concern. Billy and Lynn had a reputation for leaving a path of destruction wherever they went, but it was hard to believe that their reputation could extend to the remotest locations in Europe, but who could be sure.

"The admission is twenty zlotych," the woman said in broken English. She recognized them as Americans the moment they stepped in the door, and adapted by using her knowledge of the English language. Behind her, a girl about Luke's age peeked her blonde head out from behind a curtain leading to a back room.

Luke pulled the money from his pants pocket and handed it to the woman.

Katie cleared her throat, "We are looking for something in particular, a balance scale..."

"We have many things here," the woman replied. "Why do you search for such an object?"

"We're doing research for a school project," Katie lied. "It was invented by Soren Jacobsen; our teacher told us we could find one of his inventions here."

At the sound of Soren's name the woman immediately went cold. "What would make you ask such a thing? Soren Jacobsen was a myth; there was no such man."

"But there was," Katie replied. "He was a Danish inventor who worked in this area. This is the only museum in Wrzosowiak, and we were told that the scale was sold to a museum here. Are you sure you don't have anything?"

"I don't know who would have told you such lies, but we have nothing here by Her Jacobsen. You are best to look elsewhere."

"Are you sure? Because we have reason to believe..."

"I am sure," the woman answered abruptly. "Here…here is your money, you can leave now." With her right hand she thrust the money at Luke while guiding the kids to the door with her left. No sooner had they crossed the threshold than the door was shut firmly behind them.

"That was strange," Katie said.

Luke was about to respond when he noticed Tommy, Billy and Lynn disappear around the side of the building. "Where did they head off to?"

By the time Luke and Katie got to the corner of the building they only caught a glimpse of Billy and Lynn rounding the next corner into the alley behind the museum.

"Where can they be going?" Katie asked.

Together, Luke and Katie rushed to the next corner and peeked around the bend. There they saw Tommy speaking with the blonde girl from the museum. Billy and Lynn hovered around their feet.

Katie started to approach, but Luke held her back. "Stay back," he whispered, "let's see how this plays out."

* * *

The girl looked starry eyed at Tommy.

He swished his hair away from his face with a flip of his head and gazed in her eyes. She quickly looked away. Luke had seen this behavior before. She was smitten. If she knew anything that could help them, Tommy would have that information in no time.

"Is that your mom?" Tommy asked. He used his finger to gently raise her chin and look into her eyes.

She looked at him and exhaled deeply. "She's my Mamor... this is her museum."

"Does she know about Soren Jacobsen?"

"Are you a part of The Quest?"

"The Quest?"

"The Quest," the girl said to him as if it should be obvious. "You are searching to learn more about Soren Jacobsen?"

"If we are, is that a bad thing?"

"A bad thing? I guess it depends on why you want to know. My Mamor does not trust anyone who is a part of The Quest."

"I don't know what The Quest is, but you can trust us."

The look in the girl's eyes said it all. She wanted to trust him, no matter what he said. "We can go to my house," she offered "we may be able to help you there."

Tommy looked over his shoulder. He spied Luke and Katie peeking around the corner. He waved. "Is it okay if my brother and cousin come too?" he asked.

"Okay," the girl said with a smile. "My name is Lena," she added, extending her hand to Tommy.

"Lena?" Tommy laughed as he took her hand, "that's my mom's name."

They exchanged warm smiles, but their hands did not part.

"This is my brother Luke and my cousin Katie, and the two little ones are Billy and Lynn."

"It is nice to meet you," Lena said without releasing Tommy's hand.

"Nice to meet you too."

With Tommy's hand in hers, Lena led the group down a dirt path between two houses and away from the museum. It didn't take long for them to reach a small cottage built from stone. It had a thatched roof and was surrounded by a bramble of thorns and wildflowers.

"Mama!" Lena called, "we have company… Americans."

No sooner had the words left Lena's mouth than a woman's head popped out of one of the windows. "Lena," the woman answered with a glowing smile, "Kto jest z tobą?"

"English Mama," Lena corrected her mother. "They are American friends. This is Tommy… and Luke and Katie…and the little ones are Billy and Lynn."

"Come…come in," the woman welcomed them. Her English was not as smooth as her daughter's but she spoke it very well. "It is so nice to have guests."

They all walked into a warm kitchen, which made up most of the building. Above them was a loft with enough room for several beds.

"Please sit… I will make some coffee and biscuits."

Luke exchanged looks with Katie and Tommy.

"I don't think they drink coffee, Mama," Lena laughed. "They're Americans."

"Oh my," the woman shuddered, "we don't have any Coca Cola." In just that short of time her voice had changed. The accent that had flavored her words was already starting to fade.

"Thank you, but we don't need anything to drink," Katie offered.

"Mama, they are on The Quest."

"The Quest?!?" the woman replied. "But they are so young... and Americans... what would American children know about The Quest?"

"We don't really know anything about The Quest," Katie replied. "We came here looking for one of Soren Jacobsen's inventions."

"And what do you think The Quest is, my dear girl?" the woman laughed. "Are you wizards?"

"Wizards?" Luke questioned.

The woman looked at them, bewildered. "Perhaps I am not using the right word... how do you say... magicians... are you magicians?"

"We are studying for a class," Katie responded.

"I don't know of any school that teaches about Soren Jacobsen," the woman replied with a sharp smile, "but there are plenty of wizards who want to learn his secrets."

"Was Soren Jacobsen a magician?"

"He was many things: an inventor, an artist, an architect, an engineer. But the things he would create all had magic in them." She turned to her daughter. "What about them, do any of them have the magic?"

"Oh yes," the girl answered. Her face turned red with embarrassment.

"What does that mean?" Luke asked.

The woman answered, "All people have magic, some more than others. Some can use magic... with potions or spells. Some can use magical objects, and still others can perform magical feats by feeding off the magic around them. But some, a select few, have magic within them, it is these people that we call wizards, true magicians. They are able to create the magical objects that can be used by others. They are very rare.

"Lena here is very sensitive to the magic and can sense the magic in others."

Lena raised her finger and pointed at Tommy.

"Yes," her mother laughed, "his is very obvious."

"What do you mean?" Luke asked inquiringly.

"Do you not see it? He has charm magic. Certainly you have spent enough time with him to know this?"

Luke thought about all of the ways in which Tommy was able to charm his way through a situation. He never thought of it as magic, but he always marveled at this ability. He even envied Tommy this gift.

"And what about the rest of us?" Katie inquired.

Lena leaned over and whispered in her mother's ear.

"Not all people understand it as magic, but I don't think she will be surprised to hear it," her mother answered her.

"What? What did she say?" Katie asked.

"You have a very unique magic... the kind that leads most people to the stage. You can become anything... or anyone you want."

Luke laughed out loud. This was most certainly true. Katie had the ability to transform herself and her character to fit any situation, even in the most stressful situations. This was also something he never thought of as magic, but was certainly a gift, a gift that had served them well in many instances.

"And what about me?" Luke asked.

Again, Lena whispered to her mother.

"Your magic is more...subtle."

"Subtle? What does that mean?"

Lena offered an awkward smile.

"But you said that all people have magic."

"Just because it has not shown itself does not mean it does not exist," the woman answered. The words were meant for her daughter as much as for Luke.

Luke was disappointed and he had trouble hiding his reaction. How could everyone else have magic and he could have none? It was almost painful to think about it; just another example of not quite fitting in.

Lena's mother sensed Luke's discomfort and attempted to change the subject. "But you did not come here to talk about magic, you came here to learn about Soren Jacobsen."

30. History Lesson

Lena's mother picked herself up and moved across the kitchen to a cupboard along the wall. She opened a drawer and pulled out three tablecloths, laying them neatly at the edge of the table. She then withdrew a book, holding it close to her chest as she returned to the table and laid it out before them.

Her face glowed with anxious anticipation, like she was seeing it for the first time. "This is the foundation of 'The Quest.' It is a story that was discovered by one of the founding members and shared with everyone with a like mind, a passion for discovering the true secrets of Soren Jacobsen. It was shared with me and now I share it with you." She cleared her throat and prepared to read from the ancient text.

The following passages were passed down to me by my father, as they were passed to him by his father and his father before that, never intended to be written. I swore an oath to my father, just as my father swore to his father and every man in our lineage also swore. But alas, I have no son and I cannot, will not, let this story, this explanation, end with me. And so I put these words to text and will place them where I know they will one day be found, so that everyone may understand what we did and why, that there was a reason why things happened the way they did, that none of this was by chance, but instead by design, designed by the master, for in his infinite wisdom he understood that which most men are unable to comprehend.

Hundreds of years ago in a hidden cavern by the Sounds of the Elsinore in the town of Kronenburg and the country of Denmark, a secret meeting took place. But this was no ordinary secret meeting, this meeting was so important that no less than the fate of the whole world rest in its results. This clandestine rendezvous was between six warriors, loyal servants to the nation of Denmark. If you want to understand the quest, it is important that you know about these warriors and this secret gathering.

These warriors were childhood friends, they grew up together, they played and worked together, and together they went off to war. They had been a group of seven at that time, but after their last major battle their leader, the hero of the group, returned from the battlefield and fell into a deep sleep that no one could wake. His name was Holger Danske and he was known around the globe for his magnanimous victories in battle with his legendary sword. In this particular battle, Holger Danske had just defeated a giant, a beast among men, and a destroyer of armies. This giant, Brehus, crushed everything in his path. But the valiant Holger Danske met him in battle and defeated the mighty man.

You're probably wondering how Holger

Danske emerged victorious? The stories surrounding his victory are confusing and almost unbelievable. According to the legend, Holger Danske performed fantastic feats of power and quickness, many of which, if believed, would conflict with the laws of physics that we know today. But that is how the people who were there have told the story, and for generation upon generation those are the only accounts of the epic fight. Two things have remained constant throughout every version, and that is that Holger Danske wielded the most powerful weapon any man had ever seen, and against all odds he defeated the giant to keep the homeland safe.

When Holger Danske returned to Denmark after this epic battle, he did not go to his home village as some may have expected, but instead, retired to a hidden cavern along the coast. It is said that he entered the cavern, sat down on a throne he himself had chiseled out of the cavern wall, crossed his arms, put his chin on his chest, and fell asleep.

Now when my father first told me this story I said to myself, "Give the guy a break; he just conquered a giant, let him have his rest." But this wasn't a couple of days or even a couple of weeks. This sleep went on and on and on and on.

As you can imagine, while asleep, Holger Danske was defenseless, you can also figure that a man like Holger Danske, a hero of the Danish nation, was also the main target of every enemy.

The group of six, the warriors and Holger Danske's childhood friends, owed him their lives. He had saved each and every one of them on countless occasions and now, in his time of need, they pledged to protect him.

And so they took turns guarding their warrior leader. Around the clock, twenty-four hours a day, seven days a week, they guarded him. They passed this responsibility on to their sons who passed it on to their sons for generations. At first, they stood at the mouth of the cavern as each man took a shift. But this method would not work forever, and soon they began creating defenses around their sleeping hero. Over the years, the fortifications grew and grew with modern weaponry, buttressed walls, and battlement stations. And still, the chosen ones took turns standing guard, protecting their sleeping hero.

With each passing generation, they continued their task until the descendants of the original six considered themselves unable to fulfill the sworn duty. They were loyal at heart, but no longer fierce in battle. Their hair was now grey and their stature not nearly as imposing. Once capable of leading a battalion of men into combat, those days were gone, and they knew that their time to serve their sleeping hero was coming to an end.

And so a brilliant plan was initiated; they commissioned a legendary inventor to create special protections within the fortress, to keep enemies away from their hero after they could no longer perform the task. At the inventor's direction, they started by spreading the word that the story of the sleeping Holger Danske was a myth, that Holger Danske had died and they had created the tale to keep invading armies in fear of Denmark and its greatest warrior. They also led everyone to believe that the fortress was not his resting place, but instead, a monument to the hero and his accomplishments. For over a decade the master inventor worked in secrecy, creating the ultimate defense plan. Even the warriors themselves were not allowed to know all of the defenses he was creating.

This meeting, in the hidden cavern, was called because the work was complete and it was time to let each man know his role in securing the secrets to Holger Danske's safety. Each man came to this meeting prepared for anything, dressed for battle with chain link armor over their bodies and swords at their sides. Their uniforms were worn with pride, crisp and sharp, red with a white Scandinavian cross across the midsection, and their coat of arms, a circle of nine hearts around three lions, displayed over their hearts.

On this night, the cavern was lit only by a few torches, flickering flames that cast strange shadows across the cavern's uneven walls as much as fear and uncertainty cast strange shadows on each man's soul. Despite all of their accomplishments, each and every one of them questioned his own worthiness for this final assignment. Each man knew what needed to be done. Failure was not an option; they had been taught by their fathers that honor and integrity were more important than life itself.

In the back of this dimly lit cavern stood a stone table, and at the back end of the table sat a large monolith depicting the master, the most revered warrior, dressed for battle, helmet on his head, sword by his side, arms crossed, chin resting on his chest, eyes closed. Despite the appearance of deep sleep, he was still imposing, powerful and commanding all at once.

Jafet, the leader of the group of six, stepped forward. "Then the decision is made, we all know what needs to be done," Jafet said. He was a large brutish man with a hint of red to his otherwise graying hair and beard. The lines around his face showed his age and the steel of his eyes revealed the seriousness of their mission.

Upon Jafet's signal, all six raised their swords to join together in a single point above their heads. In their opposing hands, each held a flagon of brew, and in unison they lifted their ale, tapped their mugs and cheered, "To Holger Danske! Skol!" The metal clank of their steins echoed throughout the darkened cavern. Each man drained his mug in one long, extended draught and then slammed his empty mug onto the stone table.

"It is time to bring them in," Jafet announced.

"Even the boy?" one of the men asked. His words drew a sneer from the others. The warrior who had asked the question was the smallest of the group, bare faced and almost youthful at first glance, but upon closer inspection, aged and battle-hardened just like the rest.

"Yes, both of them Walentin," Jafet answered. "Soon we will be too old to defend our sleeping master; we can leave nothing to chance."

One of the others, Tago, a wiry man with a chiseled jaw and a patch over his left eye, left the group and crawled out of the cavern through a small hole. The others stood around in tense silence until Tago returned a short while later, followed by an old man with tangled, knotted gray hair and odd multi-lensed glasses. A young boy of five or six years with hair so blonde it looked like it had been kissed by the sun, followed close behind. The old man with the wild hair struggled to get his frame through the tiny opening. The young lad scampered in, bouncing around in boyish delight.

Struggling to straighten his old and brittle bones, the old man stood up. He brushed the dirt from his clothes. "Good day, Jafet." Turning to the others, he added, "and to you Absalon, Lage, Lasarus and Walentin."

"We are very grateful for your service,"

Walentin, the smallest of the warriors, answered. He did not make eye contact, but instead looked forlornly to the ground.

Concerned, the old man moved toward Walentin, but Jafet stepped between them. "It is time Soren; show us what you have done."

"Yes, yes," the old man responded, shaking a thought from his head and returning his attention to the task at hand. He called out to his young assistant, "Hans, dear boy, bring me the clock."

The young blonde boy scurried to a corner of the cavern and dragged out a small cart, bringing it to the edge of the table nearest to the statue. From the cart he lifted an intricate contraption to the table, struggling to support its weight.

Soren's eyes lit up when he saw his masterpiece. He rushed over and helped the boy lift the clock, sliding it into a groove on the top of the table. "This clock is the key," the old man explained. "Hans, the pieces."

Again, the young boy scampered away, this time returning with a satchel over his shoulder. As he neared the clock, the satchel began to move and shift at his side. The six men looked on in rapt anticipation.

"As I was saying, this clock is the key. And these pieces," Soren added, taking the satchel from the lad, "these pieces are to make the clock work." He opened the satchel and reached inside. The first object he removed was circular with ribbed edges and a hole in the center. With the piece in hand, he turned to one of the warriors, a man with salt and pepper hair and a scraggly beard. "This cog," he said holding up the piece, "belongs to Lage." He handed it to the warrior with the salt and pepper hair. As soon as Lage accepted the piece, it began to emit a soothing violet glow. The others looked on in disbelief.

Soren returned to the satchel. This time he removed a round coin with strange markings on the side and a hole in the center. Approaching the smallest of the warriors, he handed it to him and said, "Walentin, this coin belongs to you." As the coin passed from the old man to the young looking warrior, a yellow light emerged.

Soren repeated the process. "For you Tago, I have this rod," he said, handing the small object to the man with the patch over his left eye. As Tago took the rod, a red light emerged. Without pause, the old man returned to the satchel and withdrew a fish hook, which he handed to the tallest of the warriors, a man with a smooth bald head, but a full thick beard of gray hair. "Lasarus," he said, "this fish hook belongs to you." The fish hook took on a green glow as it touched Lasarus' hand. Returning once more to the satchel, Soren pulled out a cross. "Absalon," he said, "for you I have this cross." And when Absalon took the cross, it too lit up, only its light glowed a soft blue.

"And what about me?" Jafet, the leader, questioned.

"I did not forget you Jafet," Soren replied with a small laugh. "For you there is this," he said, pointing to the masterpiece of the collection, the clock that stood firmly at the center of the table.

Jafet's eyes lit up as he surveyed the clock in all its magnificence. Looking at it from all angles, he asked, "So how does it work?"

"Ah, that is the beauty," the old man replied. He then motioned for the others to draw near. "Reach in and touch the ring at the center," he directed Jafet.

Jafet did as he was told and when his finger touched the ring, the entire clock began to hum and lit up in a soft radiance.

Soren then directed Lage to a place inside the clock just below the ring, and said, "Insert the cog here." Lage followed the old man's direction. Soren then motioned the man with the patch over his left eye into place, the red glowing rod in his hand. As Tago inserted the rod into the hole of the cog, both pieces floated together. Then Walentin, under Soren's guidance, attached the yellow glowing coin to the other end of the rod. No one made a sound, everyone stunned by the events unfolding before them.

The old man then pointed at Lasarus. "Now you," he said. Lasarus approached with the green light of the fish hook leading the way. He placed it inside the clock, connecting one end to the coin and the other end to the cog.

Magically, the pieces hovered in the middle of the clock, each emitting its own magnificent glow, creating a rainbow of brilliant color.

The old man pointed to the blue cross in Absalon's hand. Absalon shifted forward, lifting the cross and moving it toward the center of the clock. A powerful force pulled the cross out of his hand, and it joined with the other pieces and began a strange rotation that set the gears of the clock into motion. The hands spun rapidly, and then for a brief moment, stopped. The gears started and stopped several more times, shifting levers within the clock and within the table until a loud crack echoed throughout the cavern. The walls and floor began to shake. The statue at the end of the table began to move. Instinctively, the warriors drew their swords ready for battle, but there was none. Instead, a hidden passageway was revealed.

The entire group backed away, dumfounded by what was happening. A proud smile adorned the old man's face as he watched his creation work to perfection. Stepping forward, he led them to the newly revealed passageway. Just inside the opening, he pointed to a pulley system built into the ceiling. "This will lower us down to the finished tomb," he explained.

Jafet stretched his large frame into the opening to inspect the pulley system and to look down the dark sloping shaft. He backed up and turned to Soren. "Lower the boy first."

"Of course," the old man replied. "Hans are you ready?"

The small boy jumped forward excitedly, his blonde hair bouncing with every step. Nimbly, he placed his foot into the stirrup attached to the pulley system and quickly lowered himself down the shaft to the chamber below.

The old man called down. "Light the lamps like I showed you," he instructed.

One by one, the warriors lowered themselves down the shaft.

At the bottom, they arrived at a new chamber. Unlike the primitive cavern above, this room was finely appointed with a smooth finished floor and tiled walls. Six columns surrounded the perimeter. Carved into each column was a statue, one each for Jafet, Lage, Tago, Absalon, Lasarus, and Walentin. Resting in one hand of each statue was an oil lamp--six lit lamps in all--that filled the chamber with a magnificent glow. The other hand of each statue was raised and held a sword. Together, the swords pointed upward to a beautiful mural on the ceiling designed from thousands of tiny colored tiles. It was a scene of their master, Holger Danske, lifting his sword in victory at the end of an epic battle. Together, the six warriors stood in awe, staring open-mouthed at the beauty and intricate detail of the artwork. Each of them took the time to admire the mural and the statues, marveling at the incredible likeness of the images.

At the far end of this chamber stood a replica of the statue from the cavern above, this one much larger than the original. The statues were identical, with two noticeable differences. Here the subject sat not on a chair, but on a throne, and here the table before him was set for a feast with golden goblets, plates and cutlery.

"As you will see, the table is set for eight, one for each of you," the old man said, pointing to each of the warriors and the main statue, "and one for the uninvited guest," he added, a reference to the ancient tradition.

The warriors all looked at one another with extreme satisfaction. They were truly impressed with all that the old man, Soren, had achieved. "You have done well old man," Jafet said. "This is a fitting resting place for the master."

"And secure," Soren replied. "The chamber can only be opened when all of the pieces are together with each of you."

"And the second part of our plan?" Jafet inquired.

"Each of your hiding places has been prepared," the old man explained to the group. "And I made sure that no one is aware of the others' secrets."

Jafet, the leader, looked at the others and said, "It is time." Each of the warriors exchanged a knowing glance then one by one they left the chamber using the pulley system to lift themselves back up the shaft.

The old man looked down at his apprentice. "This is my greatest masterpiece," he said with a grin. The boy returned the smile.

When the last of the warriors, Lasarus, ascended the shaft, the old man and the boy waited for the rope and stirrup to return, but it did not. Instead, they were greeted by a loud crashing sound as the pulley system from above tumbled down the shaft and landed in pieces at their feet. Jafet's booming voice soon followed.

"There is one problem," Jafet called down. "There is one person who knows all of the secret hiding places and the secrets that lay within. I am afraid that information must die with you. You have served the Master well; you shall die with honor and dignity, a tribute to the homeland." And with those words, the passageway above was sealed tight, leaving the old man, Soren, and the young boy, Hans, trapped in a cavern by the Sounds of Elsinore in the town of Kronenburg.

* * *

Lena's mother closed the book and looked at Luke and the others. They were riveted, eyes wide, ears glued to her every word. "No one knows where the pieces are hidden," she added, "but many people search for them. This story, shared by many, is the fuel for 'The Quest,' the foundation for our search."

"We believe the pieces are stored in six secret chambers around the world, and that if they could be recovered, they would reveal Curtana, Holger Danske's magical sword."

Luke looked around at the others. He clutched his bag, and Hans' journal, close to his side. It was hard to contain the secret held within. He hoped that none of the others would reveal anything, but secretly wondered what they would say if he shared what he knew with Lena and her mother.

"That is the story of The Quest." Lena's mother closed the book and showed the front cover. There it was, the image they had seen before, of the triangle with the serpent wrapped around its three sides. "The symbol for The Quest," she added, pointing to the image, "three sides of the triangle and three serpentine vines, the six pieces that together will reveal the path to Curtana."

Luke pondered the woman's words. "How do you know there are six chambers around the world?"

The woman hesitated. "The six Danish warriors," she said, "they each set out in different directions to hide the five pieces and the clock."

"But why chambers?" Luke asked. "They could have hidden the pieces anywhere."

"Mama," Lena said, "it is for 'The Quest.'" The woman shook her head, but Lena did not relent.

Luke knew at once what Lena meant. "Have you been in the chambers?" he asked.

Lena looked at her mother with pleading eyes. Reluctantly, the woman stood up and went back to the cupboard. She opened the same drawer from which she had pulled the journal. This time she lifted a false bottom from the drawer and then removed a folder. "These are photos taken from a chamber in France," Lena's mother said. "It is a museum now, but we believe it used to be the location of one of the six pieces."

Luke spread the photos out on the table. Everyone gathered to get a closer look. They recognized the photos right away, the entrance to the chamber, the dome ceiling, the alcoves, and the images on the wall. It was all there, just like they remembered, and identical to the pictures Katie had taken only a couple of days ago.

"So this was in France?" Luke asked, trying his best to sound clueless.

"Yes," Lena answered, "northern France, in the Normandy area."

"And you think there are other chambers throughout the world?" Luke said.

"Six," Lena replied, "the one in France and five others if we are correct."

"Do you think there could be one here in Czestochowa?"

"No!" Lena's mother snapped. Realizing she had reacted a little too quickly, she calmed her tone and added, "No… the six locations are in Russia, Finland, France, Italy, Greece and Denmark."

"Nothing here in Poland?" Luke inquired.

"No," Lena's mother answered. "You know, it is getting late. You children must be getting home, and Lena must do her chores before bedtime."

"Actually," Luke said. "We don't have anywhere to stay tonight. We're kind of on our own until we can get to our Uncle's house in Russia tomorrow."

She eyed them suspiciously. "You have nowhere to stay? Where are your parents? Do they know you have nowhere to sleep?"

"We were supposed to stay in the hotel they booked for us, but we decided to visit the museum and now it's too late to get the train back."

"You will stay here," the woman said resolutely. "And tomorrow we will get you to the train and back to your parents."

Luke and the others helped Lena with her chores while Lena's mother made them a dinner of pierogies and kielbasa. When they finished cleaning up after dinner, they all bundled together to sleep in the loft. Billy and Lynn fell asleep quickly, as did Tommy and Katie. But Luke stayed awake, thinking about everything he had learned that day and the last stages of their journey. Even if they didn't find the chamber, this was a big step in their quest, another piece to the Soren Jacobsen puzzle. And now there were more steps to take. They would begin tomorrow with a trip to Russia.

31. Ever Been to Moscow

"I'll never get tired of seeing Soren Jacobsen's chambers," Dad said as the limo pulled out of the cemetery parking lot and back onto the highway.

Mom frowned. "Aren't you worried about the boys?"

"They're very resourceful," Dad answered, "I'm sure they'll be okay."

"They're alone in a strange country and we have no idea where," Mom gasped.

Aunt Janine cut in, "We know where they're going. I'm going to put you on a train to Finland, you can meet them there."

"I'll feel better when they're with us," Mom responded.

"You're not coming with us?" Dad asked Aunt Janine. "There's still one more chamber to see."

"That's going to have to wait," Aunt Janine replied. "I have business to attend to."

"So this is the end of the journey?"

"For now, I'll touch base when we are all back in the States."

Mom looked at Dad, her concern was written all over her face.

"They're going to be fine," he assured her. "By the time they're done this trip they'll be seasoned travelers, ready for anything."

"That's what you said about Camp Forsyth," Mom replied.

The limo pulled up to the curb at the train station. Aunt Janine motioned to the door. Mom and Dad stepped out and the limo driver was placing their bags on the sidewalk. Mom bent over to make sure they had everything and before they knew it the limo was gone.

"Guess we don't have to worry about long tearful goodbyes," Dad joked. He turned around and saw a man in a blue uniform with an oddly shaped hat. "Excuse me sir," Dad asked the man, "can you tell us which train will take us to Finland?"

The man said nothing put pointed up a set of stairs to a platform fifty yards away.

* * *

Have you ever been to Moscow? It's an incredibly beautiful city with a lot of history. Most people think that it's cold, but not in July. In July, the days are long and the air is hot. Everyone speaks Russian in Moscow. Quite a few speak English as well, but not as much as in the other cities Luke and the others had visited on this trip.

By appearance, the kids fit right in, their clothes, their hair, their skin. But the moment they opened their mouths to speak, they stuck out like an adult in the kid's line for the Wicked Wiley roller coaster. Tommy managed to pick up certain parts of the language pretty quickly. He read the English to Russian dictionary on the train. It's one thing to learn words, a whole nother to reflect dialogue and culture.

Luke studied his brother. Tommy had more "magic" than just charm. He was big, and strong, and he could pick up

175

any language in no time at all. It didn't matter if it was Danish or French or Russian or even sign language, Tommy understood it like it was in his mind all along. These thoughts didn't set well with Luke. There was a strange, uneasy feeling growing inside of him. It was a combination of jealousy and envy.

When they got off the train in Moscow, Tommy approached a man on the train platform. "Prostite, ser," he said. "wgde nam poymat' taxi?"

The man wore a blue uniform and an oddly shaped hat. His nondescript face carried a simple look. He didn't care for his job and it showed. One look at Tommy and the others and he recognized them as Americans. He didn't bother to respond in Russian. "Go to the bottom of the stairs," he said in his best but still disjointed English, "then turn left and you will see the yellow sign."

"Spasibo," Tommy replied graciously.

Luke and the others followed Tommy down the steps, lumbering with their bags. Even though they had packed light, over time, the weight of their bags began to wear on them. It was tiresome dragging all of their belongings wherever they went.

At the bottom of the stairs they saw a long line of taxis. There was an even longer line of people waiting for their services. Luke stepped to the back of the line and dropped his pack to the ground. Katie and Tommy did the same with theirs. Billy and Lynn just allowed the weight of their backpacks to pull their bodies back onto the sidewalk where they laid on top of them, unwilling to fight gravity any longer.

Tommy sat on his suitcase and read through the English to Russian dictionary, all the while listening intently to the conversations going on around him.

Luke looked at his brothers and cousins. This whole trip was really taking its toll, the weight of their bags, the uncertainty of where they would sleep, the strange foods, the pace of life. Ever since they saw No-Neck and The Walrus in Greece, this non-stop journey had turned into a frenetic scramble. Fear of being captured kept them from following their planned itinerary and caused them to miss the beautiful hotels and plush beds that came with it. They were fortunate in Greece. The couple at the grocery store was so nice, and then again in Poland when they met Lena and her mother. But in Russia they knew no one, and their funds were running low.

How much further could they go on? Luke wasn't ready to give in, but he wasn't sure about the others. Certainly they would need a little luck. There were only two sites left to visit, and the first of those was now within reach.

The taxi line moved slowly; by the time they reached the next available cab, Tommy was ready. "My dolzhny dobrat'sya do Sarskoe," he said to the driver. This time he sounded just like every person around them. His diction and dialect were natural, the man barely took notice.

Luke marveled at how quickly Tommy had adapted.

The bags were tossed into the trunk, and the kids all piled into the cab. Tommy sat in front. Luke, Katie, Billy and Lynn snuggled into the back. In a flash, the taxi took off from the curb, weaving in and out of traffic at breakneck speed.

Outside, the landscape whizzed by. Russia, and more specifically Moscow, was unlike any of the cities they had visited before, on this trip or any other for that matter. The first thing Tommy noticed were the domes, visible in the distance, and spanning high into the sky. They looked like onions sitting on top of the buildings, bulbous bases tapering to a sharp point.

The expanse of buildings, some onion topped, others squared and broad, morphed into something completely different, a collection of walls, fortified, ready for a war that hadn't seen the streets of Moscow for many years. It was a sturdy complex that went on for miles.

In the back seat, Luke and the others couldn't appreciate the passing scenery. They were tossed like rag dolls as the car jerked back and forth. Luke screamed from beneath a pile of bodies, "Tell him to slow down, we don't want to die."

Tommy pulled out his dictionary and searched for the right words. By the time he found what he was looking for, the driver was out of the major congestion of city traffic and heading into the countryside. They were no longer weaving through cars, but they were still moving at a brisk pace.

"Vy ne dolzhny yezdit' tak bistro," Tommy told the driver.

"Ya vam sekonomit' den'gi na platnykh," the driver responded with a hearty laugh. "Vy budete delat' eto do menya v chayevykh."

Tommy quickly paged through his dictionary, trying to decipher the words he didn't understand. He shouted back to Luke and the others, "He's trying to get us there as quickly as possible... we can make it up to him on the tip."

Several minutes of highway driving brought them to an exit. The sign read "Sarskoye Gorodishche." It was a medieval fortified settlement, once used by the Vikings to protect the Volga trade route along the Sara River. Now it was a popular attraction for tourists.

The driver veered off the main road, barely slowing down for the turn. Luke and the others slid wildly across the back seat. Three more sharp turns sent the kids reeling again and again. Then the taxi came to a screeching halt in a dirt and stone parking lot.

Luke jumped from the car and knelt down, glad to be on solid ground. The others tumbled out of the vehicle.

The driver got out of the car and pulled their bags from the trunk. He turned to Tommy with his hand out.

"We need a thousand rubles," Tommy said to Luke.

"Don't you have any money left?"

"I spent it all," Tommy replied, sheepishly.

Luke fished the money from his pocket and handed it to Tommy. "Tell him to wait for us here," he said, but as soon as Tommy paid the man, the taxi was gone in a cloud of dust.

"Where is he going?" Luke yelled. "You were supposed to tell him to wait!"

"I didn't get the chance," Tommy replied.

"How are we supposed to get back?" Luke screamed. "We were counting on you."

Tommy didn't know what to say. He didn't want the guy to leave, but he was gone before he had a chance to open his mouth. Still, the look in Luke's eyes and the tone in his voice said it all.

Katie stepped forward. "There's nothing we can do about it now," she offered. "Let's just find the next site and deal with that later."

Luke rolled his eyes. "If you want something done right," he taunted.

Tommy burst out, "Why don't you just do it yourself then? You're so quick to point out my mistakes; I didn't see you talking to the driver." He was fuming, ready for a fight.

"I thought you could handle it," Luke responded. "I guess I was wrong."

Tommy took a step towards Luke, but Katie stepped in his way. "Let it go," she said. "We have things to do."

Tommy turned away, rage seething beneath his skin.

Luke seemed none the wiser. He pulled the journal from his backpack and perused the section about Moscow. "It says here we need to go to the back of the cemetery."

Everyone looked around. The cemetery was huge. It went on for miles in every direction. It was so large, it was impossible to see the end.

"Where do we start?" Katie asked. "This could take forever."

"Let's just get this over with," Tommy grunted. "If we split up, we can each begin looking."

"Don't just take off," Luke corrected him. "Let's use our brains this time."

"Whatever," Tommy retorted.

"You don't even know what you're looking for," Luke said, mockingly. "You can't solve every problem with your muscles; sometimes you have to think."

Tommy had heard enough. He started towards Luke.

Katie recognized the fury building in Tommy, and stepped in front of him. "So what are we looking for Luke?" she asked over her shoulder, never taking her eyes off of Tommy.

Luke read through the journal and then lifted his head. "First off, the journal is hundreds of years old, so we can rule out all of the areas with newer tombstones. Second, the first graves would have been placed closest to the original church; they wouldn't have gone too far if they didn't have to. And third, the journal makes reference to a mausoleum, so we need to look for an area with not just gravestones, but small buildings as well."

They started their search near the old church, each moving in a different direction.

Katie announced, "The graves here are from the early 1700's."

"These are from the 1800's," Tommy called out.

They continued their search until Luke finally spotted something. "Hey guys, come here, I think this is it."

The others came running. "How can you be sure?" Katie asked.

Luke pointed to a row of roughly hewn tombstones. "Look at these," he said, "they're so old you can't even read them."

They bent down to look. He was right. Years of the elements had rendered the stones worn to the bit.

181

Now that they had more information, they concentrated their efforts in the same area, spreading out to see what they could find.

"I think I've found something," Katie called. "Come here."

Luke rushed over. "What is it?"

"Look!" Katie pointed. "This mausoleum has the Jacobsen name on it."

Luke studied it closely. "I don't think this is it. This is spelled with an 'son;' Soren spells it 'sen.'"

"Even so," Katie replied, "I think this is it."

"The journal says that the entrance is through the site of 'J-A-C-O-B-S-E-N.' I don't think he would have misspelled his own name." Luke's words dripped with sarcasm.

Katie shrugged. "It also says we need to find the mausoleum and this is the only one in this section. Can't we at least check it out?"

"Be my guest," Luke replied, his attitude snarky and impatient.

"I will," Katie said. She pushed open the door to the small building and only barely crossed the threshold before backing out. "Luke, Tommy," she yelled excitedly, "you have to see this, come quick!"

Luke was right nearby and made it there in a flash. Tommy had wandered away, so he had to run to get there. Billy and Lynn played around a tombstone, quite content with what they were doing.

Katie passed through the door, using her flashlight to lead the way. Luke was right on her heels. In the center of the room there was a small casket, not large enough for a grown up, and barely big enough for a young child. They all shivered when they thought of what was inside.

Metal brackets lined the perimeter of the room. Each one supported a very primitive torch. Luke took one look at the layout and knew they were in the right place. He dropped to his knees and opened his backpack on the floor, pulling the journal from the main compartment. "Shine your light here; I think I've found it."

Tommy looked at Katie and rolled his eyes. *"He's* found it Katie."

Katie didn't want to start another fight, so she ignored Tommy's comment. She moved to Luke's side and directed the beam from her flashlight onto the journal.

Luke read aloud, "We need to start with the first bracket," he said, pointing to the torch on the wall just to the left of the door. "There are three possible positions: pointing up, straight out, and pointing down. Tommy, are you ready?"

"Sir, yes sir," Tommy replied.

Luke, oblivious to Tommy's sarcasm, continued to bark orders, "Adjust the first one to point down."

Tommy took the bracket in his hand and pressed down. It didn't budge at first, but he continued the pressure until it loosened from its original position and fell into place. He moved to the second bracket.

Luke continued, "Keep the second one in the up position. Move the third straight out.

Tommy moved from bracket to bracket, adjusting positions exactly as Luke instructed.

"Down, down, up, straight out, straight out, up, down, up," Luke said.

Tommy moved to the last bracket and awaited Luke's direction.

"When you move this one, it should open the door to the chamber," Luke stated excitedly. Tommy and Katie waited expectantly. Finally Luke said, "Push that bracket all the way down."

Tommy did as he was told and they all snapped their heads around, searching for something, any sign of change. Nothing happened.

"What did you do?" Luke yelled.

"I didn't do anything," Tommy yelled back.

"You had to mess something up!" Luke shouted. "The chamber should have opened."

"Check for yourself," Tommy replied. "I did everything you said."

Luke read the journal and checked every bracket. "I don't understand; that should have worked." Luke sat down and stared off into space like he always did when he was deep in thought.

"Uh Luke," Katie interrupted, "we have a problem."

"Not now, I'm thinking."

Katie was at the door looking out. "It's Billy and Lynn, they're gone."

"They're fine," Luke replied. He pulled the journal onto his lap and studied the text.

Tommy raced to the door and looked out with Katie. "Forget the journal!" he screamed. "Billy... Lynn... where are you?" he called.

"They disappear all the time," Luke responded, never taking his eyes off of the journal. "I'm sure they're fine."

Tommy moved over to Luke, grabbed the journal and slammed it shut. "You need to get your priorities straight; we need to find them."

Luke looked at his younger but bigger brother. "Fine," he said, "we'll find Billy and Lynn and then we'll figure out how to get into the chamber."

Tommy stormed out of the mausoleum. "You're obsessed with this journal. You need to take a break."

Katie and Tommy scoured the area, calling out their names. There weren't many places a couple of three year olds could hide, but as experience had shown them, if there was trouble to be found, Billy and Lynn would find it. Luke gave a half hearted effort, still consumed with why the chamber did not open.

"Hey guys, come here," Katie called.

Tommy rushed over. Luke meandered, his mind still on the journal.

"Look," Katie said, pointing to a hole in the ground, "this wasn't here before."

Before either Tommy or Luke could say anything, they heard an echo of giggles coming from below.

"Lynn... Billy... Is that you?" Katie shouted.

The giggles came back, louder this time. The sound reverberated from below.

"Luke, I think this is it; I think this is the entrance. It must have opened when we were moving the brackets, and Lynn and Billy must have fallen in."

185

Luke looked at the opening and the surrounding area. That's when he noticed the flat tombstone that hinged down into the hole. It had a name on it: "Jacobsen." "Of course," he said, "we had the instructions right. And it said the entrance was through the 'Jacobsen' site."

"So should we go down or should we pull Lynn and Billy up?" Katie asked.

Luke let loose with a huge smile. "Let's get all of our stuff and check it out."

32. The Next Step

Another chamber, another experience. All of Soren Jacobsen's sites had unique characteristics, but they all also had common traits. This one was no different. There was the domed ceiling and the stone crafted alcoves, they were trademark themes of Soren's architecture. But this one had a bubbling well in the center, and the kids quickly found that it was a natural spring with water temperature like a hot bath.

This chamber also had an altar, or at least a stone table that looked like an altar. It stood empty at the far end. Luke imagined that this is where the globe was, the one Uncle Al and Aunt Janine found, and the one they had seen at the museum in Greece.

The domed ceiling in this chamber was a little different. It had the same engineering design, but the artwork on the ceiling was very intricate, with various shades of brown and splotches of blue. At the bottom ridge of the dome, near where the dome met the floor, there was the familiar horizontal line wrapped in a vine. It ran the entire way around the room.

Billy and Lynn grabbed some loose gravel from the floor and threw it into the well. They giggled as the water splashed and bubbled.

Katie took out her camera and photographed every detail. Tommy used his flashlight to give her the best view.

Luke studied the artwork on the ceiling. "What is it?" he asked himself. He tried to find a pattern, or a starting point, or some other clue that would help him figure out what it all meant. It was a flowing change of color, mostly different shades of brown with intermittent splashes of blue. It was a puzzle, he was sure. But how could he solve it?

Katie approached. "I think I got it all," she said, holding up her camera. "What do you say we get out of here and get something to eat?"

"Did you get the ceiling?" Luke asked. "All of it? I think there's something special about it."

"I got it," Katie reassured him.

They gathered all of their things and walked to the entranceway. It had been a slide coming down, but there was a ladder, leading back up. At the base of the ladder there was a lever, and when Tommy shifted it, the entrance above sealed shut. When he shifted it again, it opened. "Cool," he said. He tried the lever several more times before Katie stopped him.

"We get the picture," she laughed.

They reached the top of the ladder and were greeted by drops of rain. They scurried over to the mausoleum to close the entrance and it really started coming down.

Luke turned to Katie. "What do you say we stay in the chamber tonight? We wouldn't have to pay for a hotel room, and we'd be out of the rain?"

"What about food?" Katie asked.

"I still have some snacks from the train," Luke offered.

"Sounds good to me," Katie said.

They shifted all the brackets to reopen the chamber and raced across to the entrance. The rain poured down even harder. They scurried into the hole and Tommy sealed them in with a shift of the lever. "I guess it's good we didn't have the taxi wait for us after all," he added.

"Even a blind squirrel finds a nut some days," Luke replied.

Katie stepped between them to keep Tommy from going berserk.

The tension was still high, but when Luke brought out the food, the mood lightened. Tommy scarfed down a prepackaged Danish and half a loaf of bread. Katie chose a package of peanuts and a can of generic cola. Billy and Lynn were more interested in the water spring in the center of the room.

"Can we go in?" Lynn asked.

"Stay out of the water," Luke answered robotically, staring at the domed ceiling and trying to figure out what it meant.

"You know," Katie offered, "it might not be a bad idea. None of us has had a shower in a while; this might be the only chance we get to clean up."

"Fine," Luke replied, "just don't put your head under the water, you don't know what kind of bacteria lives in there."

Katie turned to Tommy. "Do you mind checking it out before we let them get in?"

"I'll get my clothes all wet," Tommy protested.

"Put on shorts," Katie replied. "I promise I won't look."

Tommy switched into a pair of shorts and tested the natural hot spring. "Wow, it's really warm… and there's a ledge to sit on." He helped Billy and Lynn into the water and soon all three of them were splashing around, having a good time. Katie decided to join them while Luke continued to study the ceiling. They stayed in the hot spring for a long time. By the time they got out, their skin was wrinkled like prunes. For the first time in days, they were clean and relaxed. It felt good. The time in the water really tired them out and they were ready to rest. Everyone chose a spot on the floor. It wasn't comfy like a hotel bed, but they were safe and out of the rain.

33. End of the Rope

Luke was already up by the time the others awoke in the morning. At least they thought it was morning; there was no natural light to be certain. Everyone was rested but hungry.

Luke studied the ceiling. He stood up and moved his lantern for a closer look. "It's a map," he said excitedly.

Only Katie seemed to show any interest. "Yeah," she said.

"It's leading us to Denmark... Kronborg, to be exact."

"That makes sense," Katie responded. "So is that what you've been doing all night?"

"I studied the ceiling, and the maps, and the guide books," Luke answered. "There's a train station in Rostov Yaroslavsky. It's a couple of miles from here. We should be able to walk there in about an hour."

It was still raining outside. By the time they made it to the train station they were soaked, and the tensions returned. Any good feelings from the hot spring were washed away.

The train ride from Rostov Yaroslavsky to Finland was filled with lots of awkward silence. It was all too much to handle. A week of running and hiding, with not much food, and scraping to get by, is enough to make strong men wither, but it will make little kids fall apart. Billy and Lynn fell apart; they were cranky and unbearable. The excitement of the trip was gone. All that was left were exhaustion and impatience.

"They can't take any more of this," Katie said to Luke, pointing to Lynn and Billy. The two of them were sitting on the ground, emitting a constant whine. "*I* can't take

191

any more of this," she added. Her hair was a straggly mess, her clothes tattered and torn.

"She's right, Luke," Tommy added. He too looked like he had been through Armageddon. His clothes were filthy, his normally surfer blonde hair dirty brown and matted to his head.

"What do you want me to do about it?" Luke yelled. "We don't have any money and even if we did, we're just kids, it's not like they rent hotel rooms to kids."

"There is another option," Katie said softly.

"You just want to give up? You want to quit? We've made it so far and we're almost there. If we give up now, we'll never get to finish the journey," he said, holding up Hans Jacobsen's journal.

"We don't even care about that anymore," Tommy responded. "We're wet, we're tired, we're hungry and we just want to go home."

Katie nodded her agreement. Billy and Lynn looked up from their spot on the floor with pleading eyes.

"We're not giving up," Luke stated emphatically. "*I'm* not giving up. You guys want to quit when we're this close? Come on, are you really that weak? That's pathetic."

Katie was stung by the words. "We're not pathetic... we've been through a lot and..." she pointed to Billy and Lynn, "they're only three."

"You're using them as an excuse," Luke taunted. "They'd go on if we told them to. You're the one giving up."

"Luke," Tommy interjected, "we need to rest, we need to eat, we need to dry off and get clean."

"All this time you've forced me to make every decision. Well now I'm making it!" Luke shouted. "We have one more site to visit. Once we do that, then you guys can quit, but until then, we're pushing on."

"We're not going!" Katie shouted right back. "How's that? And it's not like we wanted you to make the decisions, it's that you're too much of an arrogant jerk if we don't let you be in charge!" She had venom in her words and fire in her eyes.

"Yeah," Luke replied, "and where would you be without me? You'd be at ballet camp," he said with a point toward Katie, "and you'd be at Camp Forsyth," he added, pointing at Tommy. "Neither of you would have done anything if it wasn't for me; you'd still be living your pointless lives. We've almost solved this mystery, and it's because I've pushed us."

"We haven't solved anything if you haven't noticed," Katie yelled back. "We've seen a bunch of cool places, but we really don't know anything more than when we started."

Luke tried to say something. He wanted to dispute Katie's last statement, but he wasn't exactly sure what they had learned, except that Katie and Tommy have special gifts and he doesn't. But he wasn't about to say that.

"Fine, quit then. I'll check you into the hotel on our itinerary. It's all paid for. You can take your chances with Aunt Janine's goons, but I'm going on my own. I don't need losers like you slowing me down."

"Who are you calling a loser?" Tommy shouted.

Katie cut him off, "Let him go. Let's just get to the hotel."

The walk to the hotel was short, but the silence was so consuming it made it seem much longer. Even Billy and Lynn were abnormally quiet. When they got to the front of the hotel, Luke moved towards the door.

"You can just leave," Katie told him. "We don't want to slow you up."

"I told you I'd get you in, and I'm gonna do what I said," Luke said. "I live up to my promises. I'm not a quitter." He crossed the lobby and spoke with the woman behind the counter. It was the first time he had taken the initiative when checking into a hotel. But he had so much anger in his veins, he didn't even think about being intimidated by the situation. He just said what he had to say and checked into the room.

He came back with two keys. "You're in room 225," he said. "See ya." He left them in front of the hotel, storming away to complete his mission.

34. One More To Go

Luke strutted out of the hotel and down the street. He needed to get away from Tommy and Katie and all of their negativity. He was so close to finishing this journey and there was no way he was going to stop now. As he continued on his way, the weight of the whole situation began to wear on him.

A fight can take a lot out of you. Physical fights leave you battered and bruised. This one was mental, emotional, and it left Luke completely drained. He felt beat up both inside and out. To have both Katie and Tommy attacking him the way they did was too much.

They didn't understand. Everything he was doing was to help them, to make sure this trip was a success. They were in the middle of a huge mystery, and the more they understood, the better prepared they would be for whatever was to come next. All they could fixate on were a few negative words and a few harsh comments. This was a matter of life and death. Didn't they realize that?

These thoughts raced through his brain as he continued on his way. Steps turned into blocks, blocks turned into miles. Before Luke knew it, he was far away from the hotel and all of those problems. The neighborhood changed, but some things still looked the same. It didn't really matter; it wasn't like he had any plans of going back. They didn't want to see him, and he certainly didn't want to see them.

When Luke finally picked up his head to figure out where he was, he was standing in front of the Briggittine Convent, the location of Soren Jacobsen's last chamber.

Luke looked around. He had been so consumed inside his own head, he was oblivious to his surroundings. Then, he spotted a face he had only seen once before, but it was seared into his memory. From the black straggly hair, to the intense blackened eyes, to the scar that ran down the side of his face, Luke would never forget that image as long as he lived. Fear pulsed through his veins like lightening trapped in a bottle. His body began to shake.

Yousef saw him at the same time, and the two of them froze, each one waiting to see what the other would do.

Luke broke from his trance, bolting down a nearby alley, trying to get away as fast as he could. He didn't know the area and hoped that he could find somewhere to hide or someone who could provide protection. The alleyway was secluded. The walls on either side were solid stone. In retrospect, choosing an alley to run into was not the best idea, but there was nothing he could do about that now.

Footsteps rose up behind him. Luke turned to see Yousef round the corner. His pulse quickened, sweat dripped from his brow.

What would Yousef do if he caught him? The last time they met, he punched Luke so hard he couldn't breathe. He was bruised for a week. This time Luke didn't think he would be so lucky. Yousef approached slowly.

Luke was trapped. The alleyway ended at a wooden fence. It was too tall to climb and too sturdy to break. There was a gate, but it was locked. He looked around and spied a door for the convent. He tried the handle; it was locked.

Yousef's heavy footsteps pounded closer and closer.

Luke didn't have the nerve to look. Adrenalin took over and he did the only thing he could. He broke the glass, reached through, and unlocked the door.

The room was a basement storage area, dark and secluded. Luke found a shelf and tipped it over, blocking the door. He searched for another way out, but there was none. He ducked behind a box, looking for any place to hide.

No sooner had Luke slid in to the corner than a loud crash made him jump. Yousef reached the door and smashed his way through. The first kick shifted the door and the shelf behind it. The shelf wedged itself between the door and the opposite wall, temporarily blocking the way. Yousef kicked again, and then again. On the fourth attempt, his force was so great the door flew open and splinters of wood rained down on every part of the room.

It was over.

There was no hiding place good enough to escape the wrath of this mad man. Luke tried to stay still, but he couldn't control his nerves. His heart raced. It was hard to breathe. What could he do? All rational thoughts escaped. This man was intent on killing; he was too strong to stop, and too crazed to convince.

Yousef stepped forward and in one swipe, crushed the box that provided Luke his only cover. There was pure hatred in the man's eyes. "Today you die!" Yousef screamed. He lifted his fist, ready to pounce.

Luke didn't know how, but something inside of him willed him to stand. He clenched his fists and assumed a fighting position. Uncle Brian had taught him well. He was afraid, but also determined. He would not to go down without a fight.

Yousef laughed, and when he did, Luke surprised him. He tossed a handful of gravel into his face. With Yousef temporarily blinded, Luke followed with a right kick to the knee and then a chicken kick to the groin. It was the hardest Luke had ever kicked anything.

Yousef didn't flinch. Instead he reached forward, grabbed Luke by the throat and lifted him off the ground. "Now I will kill you, and then I will kill your brothers."

35. At Death's Door

Luke heard the words. They stirred a fire within him, but what could he do? Yousef's grip was too strong. It cut off his windpipe, his ability to breathe. In a matter of moments, he was going to pass out.

Yousef pulled him close. The stench of his breath overwhelmed Luke's nostrils. "I do this in the name of the prophet," the man growled.

Luke felt his eyes rolling back in his head. He struggled to remain conscious. Visions raced through his mind, images of Yousef's crazed eyes and scowling lips. A light reflected off of the jagged scar that ran down the wild man's cheek. Was there movement in the room? Was someone else there? Or was this a final hallucination before all conscious thought left his brain?

"Who broke my door?" a voice asked, "and what are you doing to that boy?"

Yousef dropped Luke to the floor and turned to face the man. "This doesn't concern you," he spat; "leave us alone."

Laying on the floor, gasping for breath, Luke struggled to lift his head, barely able to make out what was happening.

"You don't belong here," the unknown man said. "This is a house of God." The man raised a long weapon. It could have been a sword, or perhaps a gun. Luke couldn't tell.

Yousef was faster than either Luke or the man would have guessed. He kicked the weapon from the man's hands and wrestled him to the floor. The man kicked and shouted, but Yousef pounced, releasing a torrent of blows to the man's body and head.

Luke gasped for breath. He knew he needed to do something. His life depended on it. It took all the energy he had, but he brought himself to his feet and moved towards the door.

Freedom was a step away, but he couldn't bring himself to leave. This man saved his life. Luke couldn't abandon him. He turned, grabbed the first thing he could lay his hands on, a shovel laying on the floor, and used all of his might to club Yousef on the back of the head. The mighty villain fell with a thump.

"Come on," Luke yelled, "we have to get out of here."

The man struggled to his feet. Together they moved out the door.

Luke urged him on, "We have to run; he won't stay down long." Sure enough they heard rumblings from the storage room. Yousef was picking himself up.

"We need to call the police," Luke said.

"They won't get here in time," the man replied. He directed Luke through the now open gate at the back end of the alley.

"Then we need some place to hide," Luke implored.

"It's you we need to hide," the man explained. "It's you he's after." The man took Luke by the hand and led him towards the convent. They rushed past the building and into a courtyard. There was a small collection of tombstones and a mausoleum in the center. "Inside," the man instructed.

"But he'll find us."

"Inside," the man insisted.

Luke stepped inside the small building. The man closed the door behind them and placed a bar across the door. He hobbled around the room, lighting candles.

The inside of the mausoleum was hard to see with the dim lighting, but Luke made out six pillars supporting the roof, three on each side. In between each pillar, in the center of the wall, was a mariner's compass. A solid stone altar took up the space in the center of the room. It could easily have passed for a casket.

As more and more candles were lit, Luke got a better look at the man. He had cuts and bruises on his face and he dressed in all black. Around his neck he wore a white collar. "You're a priest?"

"There's no time for that now," the man replied. He was done lighting candles, and now rushed around the room, adjusting the compass dials along the walls. When he turned the last dial into place, the stone altar in the center of the room shifted to reveal a set of steps leading down into the earth. "Go down," the man instructed.

Luke was shocked. This was the entrance to Soren Jacobsen's hidden chamber. This man knew about it. He was using the chamber to protect Luke.

Together they descended the steps. When they reached the bottom of the stairs, the man shifted a lever and the opening above slammed shut, leaving them in complete darkness.

Luke pulled a lantern from his pack and turned it on. This room, this chamber, it looked like a church. Various thoughts flooded Luke's mind as his feet carried him deeper into the chamber.

He hadn't been to church since this whole trip began. All his life, he never missed mass, not on Sundays, not on holy days. You could set your watch to the event. Going to church was a family ritual, and now he hadn't been to church in weeks. He didn't know where Mom and Dad were, and neither Katie nor Tommy would even speak to him. Thoughts barraged his mind. He tried to block it all out, to redirect his attention to Soren Jacobsen's chamber.

It was enormous. The first thing that struck him was the height of the cathedral ceiling. How far underground were they? It made him feel small. He noticed beautiful stained glass images high on the wall. There was one of Mary, the blessed mother, one of Joseph, and another of Jesus on the cross. They looked down on him.

Luke couldn't block out the thoughts any more, something about the images forced him to look within himself. He didn't like what he saw. Thoughts bombarded him from all angles, not the thoughts that had been racking his brain, about how Tommy and Katie had been treating him, but instead, thoughts focused on everything he had done: the words he had spoken, the harshness in his voice, and his impatience with mistakes. All at once, a groundswell of emotion rushed upon him, overwhelmed him. He couldn't take it. His head began to spin. He stumbled and collapsed to the floor. The flood of feelings came to the surface so fast he couldn't hold back the tears. What was happening? No matter what it was, he couldn't explain it and he couldn't stop it.

36. Time to Make Amends

"I'm sorry," Luke whispered. He hadn't meant to say it out loud; the words escaped his lips, but they had a cathartic effect. They gave him hope that things could get better. He repeated them again only this time louder, "I'm sorry." So much was surging through his mind, so much stress, so much pressure. He said the first thing that came to his mind, "I'm sorry." Those two simple words lightened the dark cloud that shadowed his soul.

He raised his head and looked towards the altar. "I'm sorry," he said again, this time louder and with conviction. One more time he said it, "I'm sorry," but this time a voice answered him.

"This place has that effect on people." It was the man who saved him, the priest. "But sometimes it is not enough to say you're sorry; sometimes redemption requires action."

"I don't know what to do," Luke said.

The man offered a gentle smile. "Remember, it is never too late to do the right thing."

Luke nodded his head. A strong realization came to him. It wasn't enough to say the words in an empty church. He needed to say them to the people who meant the most to him. Would Tommy and Katie even listen? He wasn't sure, but he had to find out.

He looked one more time to the altar and around the room. There was more to study here in Soren Jacobsen's last chamber, but it would have to wait. There were more important things that needed to be done. "I need to get out of here," he said to the man. "Can you help me?"

"There is another way out, and it will take you out on the other side of the complex, away from that man." The priest led him to the opposite side of the chamber and up a set of steps behind the stained glass windows. They emerged in a small church on the opposite side of the convent complex.

Luke left the building and headed up the street. First he walked, and then he jogged until his body broke into a full sprint. The return was much further than he realized; it was almost an hour of running before the hotel finally came into view.

At the sight of the hotel, Luke slowed his pace to catch his breath and gather his thoughts. What exactly was he going to say? How could he make everything better?

When the cool air of the lobby hit him, a chill went up his spine. This was no time to have second thoughts; he needed to see this through. He needed to make things right. He marched through the lobby, and when the elevator wasn't there, he bolted to the stairwell, taking the steps two at a time. At the second floor, he bounded into the hallway and down to room 225.

He knocked on the door, out of breath, anxious for the opportunity to make things right. When the door opened, you could have knocked him over with a feather. It wasn't Tommy. It wasn't Katie. It wasn't even Billy or Lynn. There, standing before him, was... Mom.

Under different circumstances he would have been thrilled to see her; he hadn't seen her in weeks. But at this moment he wanted, no *needed*, to see Tommy and Katie. They were nowhere to be seen.

"Luke! Thank the Lord you're safe," Mom said. She took him into her arms and gave him a hug. It seemed like it would last forever.

Luke was stunned, so stunned he forgot to hug back. It didn't matter. Mom wrapped him so tight she couldn't tell the difference.

"Where are Tommy and Katie?" he managed to ask.

"Half way home by now," Mom explained. "Your Dad needed to get back, so they left this morning. I stayed behind to wait for you." Mom's smile was so big it gave Luke a feeling of warmth inside, a feeling he didn't deserve. There was something he needed to do, and his mind wasn't going to rest until it was done.

"I already packed your bags," Mom explained, "not that you had that much to begin with. What do you say we head to the airport and get you home?"

Luke must have said yes, but he couldn't remember. The time from the hotel to the airport was a blur. He was in such a state of shock he could hardly comprehend anything that was going on around him. It wasn't until they got to the airport and were waiting for their flight that the questions started to form in his mind.

"Where have you guys been?' he asked. "Why weren't you home when we got there? Why were you hanging out with Aunt Janine?"

"Whoa," Mom said with a laugh. "One question at a time."

Luke just stared at his mother. He had asked the questions he wanted to ask; it was her turn to talk.

"A lot has happened over the past month," Mom explained. "There's been a lot going on in our lives, and your father and I needed some answers."

"The last month?" Luke questioned, "You mean you planned all this? Before we went to Camp Forsyth?"

"Speaking of that, young man," Mom said, "why aren't you at camp? And what are you doing all alone here? And how did you pay for all of this?"

The look on Luke's face made it clear it wasn't his turn to answer questions.

"Fine," Mom replied, "but we are going to discuss it, you should not have left camp, and you definitely should not have used our credit card to book a trip around the world. Do you know how much that costs?"

Luke said nothing, but continued his penetrating stare.

"We sent you to Camp Forsyth to keep you safe," Mom said. "We couldn't leave you home all alone."

"You're working with Aunt Janine?"

"Oh dear," Mom gasped. "Yes, we went together... we wanted to learn more about Soren Jacobsen and his prophecies and we figured she was the best resource to get us where we wanted to go."

"But your credit cards weren't used... and your cell phones were still at home."

"Your Aunt Janine paid for everything; we didn't need to use our credit cards. We left our cell phones behind because we don't have international service."

Luke was struck dumb, completely speechless. "But…" he tried to say, but no words formed in his mind.

"You probably want to know where we went," Mom said.

"Uh… okay," Luke replied, still confused.

"We followed Hans Jacobsen's journals," Mom explained. "We went to France, then Italy, Greece, Poland, and then Russia."

If Luke was shocked before, it was nothing compared to how he felt now. They were following the same path, probably only a couple of days apart.

"But why?"

"We wanted to figure out what it all means, why Curtana ended up with you and why the other swords have reappeared."

"And what did you find?" Luke asked.

"A whole lot of dead ends I'm afraid," Mom said, not quite ready to reveal what they truly had learned. "We went to every location and studied everything we could, but nothing seemed to make sense." She felt a pang of guilt about leaving out the information on the Sword of the Prophet and Aunt Janine's offer to take Curtana, but now was not the right time for that.

Luke knew exactly what she meant, he too had gone to all of those places and studied everything he could, but as much as he learned, he wasn't sure he felt any closer to the answer.

Their conversation was interrupted by an announcement over the loud speaker. Their flight was boarding; it was time to go home. Together, they gathered their bags and headed for the plane. Nothing more was said. Luke was too confused to talk, and Mom was too busy making sure they had all of their belongings and their tickets.

37. Returning Home

Luke sat down on the plane and watched the other passengers file by. It was a diverse group: businessmen with their laptops, a couple of families shuttling their children to the back of the plane, all the while trying to manage more carry-on bags than should be allowed, a group of elderly ladies who stopped right at Luke's side and debated, in a rather loud and obnoxious way, which of their bags should go in the upper compartment and which should go under the seat. Luke quietly wished that all of the commotion would stop so he could be alone with his thoughts.

Mom tapped him gently on the arm. "Do you mind if I sleep on the flight? This trip has been exhausting."

Luke turned his attention away from the bickering ladies and looked at his mother. He was glad she wanted to sleep; he didn't think he could handle fourteen hours of her penetrating questions. He offered a silent nod and a smile. As she turned to rest her head against the window, a single, solitary thought came to his mind, *Where do we go from here?*

The mystery of Soren Jacobsen was incomplete. There was something he was missing. He pulled out his backpack and sorted through everything he had collected on the journey, trying to make sense of it all.

The brochures from the museums were the first things that Luke came across. He perused all of the pamphlets. Mostly they were general promotional items, but in a couple of cases there were specific details related to Soren Jacobsen. Luke committed all of the facts and details to memory.

Next came his journal entries. At the end of each day Luke took time to write down everything that he had seen and experienced. In some cases the notes were explicit, and others, when they spent more time running for their lives than relaxing in a hotel room, the notes were sparse. Again, Luke committed all that he could to memory, trying to process the significance of every detail, to figure out how it all connected.

The final source of intel came in the form of Katie's camera. The disk on her camera held up to two thousand images, and based on the volume of photos on the disk, she tried to fill every bit of available space. There were pictures of the hotels they had stayed in, pictures of Billy and Lynn playing, pictures of restaurants they had eaten at, and most importantly, pictures of every chamber they visited. One by one, Luke studied every photo.

He had to give it to her. Katie didn't miss a single detail. She photographed everything, no matter how minor it may have seemed. She had pictures of murals on the wall, tiles on the floor, even cracks in the ceiling. Luke started to get weary looking at picture after picture. Finally, he decided to put everything away and let his mind rest.

There was no way. He may have been tired, but his brain was not going to let him sleep. He turned to Mom and asked, "Would it be okay if I use your iPad?"

She didn't bother to open her eyes. "Sure honey," she replied, "it's in my bag beneath the seat."

Luke bent over and pulled the bag out from under the seat. He opened it up and withdrew the iPad. It felt strange in

210

his hand. For as long as he could remember, he played on some electronic device every day, and yet now it had been weeks since he last touched any kind of game.

He turned it on and started flipping through the various games. As much as he thought he wanted to play, his mind kept returning to Soren's secrets, everything he had learned, and all the things he had yet to discover. He was about to put the iPad away when his thumb brushed the Photos icon. Mom's collection of pictures popped up. The first image was from the chamber in Russia. Luke recognized the map on the dome ceiling right away. "I didn't realize you were taking pictures everywhere," he said, but she was sound asleep.

Luke scrolled to the beginning. He started with the first of Mom's images. He had seen these before on Katie's camera. It was the chamber in France; there were pictures of the entrance, the artifacts in the display cases, and the images on the walls. There seemed to be a lot of photos of an image Luke hadn't given much thought to: of three flags--one black, one red and one white.

It was amazing how similar Mom's photos were to the pictures on Katie's camera. He had studied Katie's photos so intently, he felt that he knew them by heart. While he had seen all of these things before, it was still exciting to relive the experience.

A group of pictures in the middle caught his attention. They were familiar, but not from this trip. "Mom," Luke said to his mother with a slight poke to her arm, "did you go back to Roland's tomb?" He asked the question, but he didn't need a response. He had all the proof he needed in the photos on the iPad. He passed through the images quickly, hardly taking any notice, until something interesting caught his eye. Mom had taken close up shots of the mural on the domed ceiling within Roland's theater in France. There were pictures of the Billy image, of Kerri, and of Greta's little sister, Hannah. Luke studied these closely, still amazed at how Soren Jacobsen could have known what they would look like hundreds of years later. Then there was that image again, of the three flags. What does that mean? Any why was it in all of the chambers? Luke thought to ask Mom, but she was in deep sleep mode.

The next images were completely new, photos of a chamber he had never seen before. His interest piqued. Here before him was a whole new set of data to flood his brain, to absorb and process.

It started with a tunnel. The images were dark and he couldn't make out much, but he could tell they were underground, and the tunnel was well constructed. The next image was inside a chamber, similar to two of the chambers he had been in before--one in Argentina and another in France. Just like the others, this one had a domed ceiling and a mariners compass dial in the center of the floor. But there was something different; this chamber was more... elegant.

The next image said it all. Aunt Janine held Soren Jacobsen's fully functioning clock, preparing to use it to open another secret chamber. Two more photos and there it was: an opening in the middle of the floor that led down a stone staircase into the unknown. Luke felt the anticipation as if he were there. Quickly, he paged through more slides. They showed steps and stone walls. It might have seemed trivial to some, but to Luke they only added to the anticipation. He needed to know what was at the bottom of these stairs.

The answer came with the very next picture.

There was no doubt that this was the chamber of a king, King Charlemagne to be exact. Everything was royal and palatial in its presentation. The grandeur was unmistakable. "You went to King Charlemagne's chamber?"

Luke wished there was video; he wished there was sound. He wanted more, to see everything they saw, to hear everything they heard. Then something caught his eye, something familiar. It was an image of a dashing young man with blonde hair, muscular shoulders and a beaming smile. Luke would know that face anywhere. It was Tommy. He was older in the image. He had a hint of stubble on his face, but it still managed to capture his everlasting charm. It was amazing how Soren Jacobsen had managed to create an image from the future with such vivid accuracy. It gave Luke mixed feelings. His mind immediately went back to Lena's mother in Poland and the connection to this mystery for everyone but him.

He dwelled on the image longer than he should have, but it was hard to break away.

When he finally slid to the next photo, he was greeted by an image of the three flags, and at the bottom left corner of the photo, a slanted line with a serpentine vine wrapped around it. It was the same line he had seen before, only slightly different. This one slanted down and to the left while the ones he had seen before slanted down and to the right. And then an image flashed in his mind. His pulse raced as the thought surged through his brain.

Quickly, he paged back through the other photos until he found what he was looking for, on the photo of the image of Billy, on the domed ceiling of Sir Roland's theater, another line with a vine wrapped around it, only this one ran horizontal.

Luke opened a drawing app on the iPad and began to doodle. First he drew the line slanting down to the left, then the line slanting down to the right and then the horizontal line. He added the serpentine vines and then began moving them around on the palette. These three images burned in his brain. He tried different patterns until he noticed a familiar image. A symbol he had seen before: at the museum in Greece, and the woman's necklace in Poland, and on the book at Lena's house. It was "The Quest" coming to life before his eyes. Why hadn't he seen it before? It was amazing how close Lena and her mother really were, so close and yet so far away. The three sides with the serpentine vines didn't represent the six magical pieces, they represented the three swords: Curtana, Joyeuse, and Durendal.

All at once, he understood. The three swords were powerful in and of themselves, but together they were something more.

Luke's thoughts returned to the magic within Katie and Tommy. Was he supposed to have Curtana? Or was it really Katie and Tommy who were the central part of Soren Jacobsen's inventions? He needed them now more than ever, not only as brother and cousin, but also as friends. He wished he could apologize right at that moment, but he was thirty thousand feet above the Atlantic Ocean, still hours from his opportunity to make amends.

38. Unfinished Business

Things were icy with Tommy when Luke got home. He thought his apology would set things straight, but some wounds run much deeper. He knew he had been wrong, but he wasn't the only one who said hurtful things, was he? Luke wasn't sure what to think or what to do. So much self-doubt crept into his mind, it was impossible to think straight.

All this time it was clear that Tommy had a gift. Katie's was so obvious everyone knew she was magical. But could it be possible that Luke was just along for the ride? It seemed ludicrous. If it wasn't for Luke, they never would have done half of the things that brought them this far. But if it wasn't for Tommy and Katie's special gifts, they never would have survived the countless perils that Luke's plans put them in.

One thing was certain. This mystery didn't end here. The question was: what was the next step? And, was Luke the right person to pursue it?

Everything else aside, Luke wanted to be a part of this adventure. He had come too far; no one was going to tell him he couldn't, even if it meant going out on his own.

He approached Tommy in their room. "I'm going to Argentina," he said in a solemn tone.

"Have fun," Tommy responded, barely acknowledging his brother's existence.

"I thought you might want to go."

"With you? I doubt it."

215

"Listen, I know I said some things... and you said some things as well... but we've been through worse."

"You listen," Tommy said, "you're still my brother and we share a room, so we're going to see each other and all, but that doesn't mean I have to like it and it certainly doesn't mean I have to follow your orders. If you want to go to Argentina then go, but I don't want anything to do with you or your stupid plans."

Luke couldn't say he didn't expect this response, but that didn't make him feel any better. At least now he knew where they stood.

*   *   *

The walk up Katie's front steps was difficult. They hadn't had the fight that he and Tommy had, but things were definitely awkward between them ever since Moscow. Luke knew he said many of the things that he did because he couldn't stand the fact that they had special powers and he was just an ordinary kid. They could never understand what it was like to sit back and watch them shine, all the while knowing that they were special and he wasn't.

Knock, knock, knock! Katie pulled the door open before his hand finished the last knock.

"What is it Luke?" she asked with a tone of disdain.

"I wanted to ask you something," Luke replied.

"We've spent a lot of time together over the past couple of weeks... too much time," Katie said. "I think we need some time apart."

"I'll be quick."

216

"What I meant to say was *I* need some time apart… I really don't want to be near you right now."

Luke choked on his next words. There was really no point in asking Katie to go to Argentina if she didn't even want to be in the same room with him. He realized the futility of the effort, but he still had something he wanted to say. "I just wanted to say I'm sorry… I said some hurtful things that I didn't mean." Luke paused as if he was going to say something else, but then turned on his heel and walked down the steps.

Katie watched him go. "That's just it Luke," she called after him. He stopped and turned back to look at her. "You did mean it… what you said to Tommy and what you said to me… you meant it. I know you're frustrated by what the woman in Poland said, but she was just a crazy old bat spouting gibberish. If you can't handle it then that's your problem not ours."

Luke started to say something, but before the words could form in his mouth, Katie closed the door. The walk home was filled with many thoughts, about what Katie said, about what the woman in Poland said, about how Luke felt, and about where this journey would go next. By the time he reached home, he was so confused he wasn't sure what to think. One thing hadn't changed, and that was his desire to take the next step, with or without his brother and cousin.

He wasn't prepared for what happened next. When he walked in the front door he was greeted by a strange sight, Mom standing in the center of the living room, a suitcase at her feet and an envelope in her hand. "I think it's time we take a trip."

"How did you...?"

"I'm just as much a part of this as you are," she replied with a wry smile. She held out her iPad. On the screen were the photos that Mom had taken during their expedition. "I've been looking at all of these and I noticed the pattern in the photos that you tagged. But there's something missing."

"In Argentina," Luke replied.

"Probably," Mom said. "That's the last of the locations and the only one you don't have photos for."

"That's what I was thinking."

"But if we're going to do this then we need to be careful."

"Of course," Luke responded. For the first time in a week, his lips formed a smile. He felt a lightness in his heart that he couldn't explain.

39. Next Stop Argentina

It was different travelling with Mom. With Mom, Luke wasn't in charge. Mom decided where they would stay, and how and when they would do things. She decided when they would eat and what they would have. She even told him when he should go to sleep. He didn't like it. Throughout this entire journey, he was the one who spent countless hours studying and preparing, learning and figuring things out. This was his adventure. He wasn't about to let someone else take over, even if it was his mother.

By the time their heads hit the pillow in the hotel in Buenos Aires, Luke had made up his mind. In the morning, he was breaking out on his own. It would be better to go it alone than to follow in someone else's footsteps.

* * *

Luke snuck out of bed before the sun rose and quietly got dressed. He packed all of his things in a backpack and slipped out of the room without making a sound. A slight pang of guilt built up in his chest, but he forced it out of his mind and moved on.

The lobby of the hotel was deserted with the exception of a sole attendant behind the check-in counter. Luke gathered his confidence and approached the woman.

"Can you help me?" he asked. "I need to rent a car."

She offered a genial smile. "I'm sorry, but you are not old enough to rent a car here in Buenos Aires," she responded.

Her tone was sweet and motherly, if not a little condescending.

Luke had watched Katie in these scenarios so many times before. He thought to himself, *If* you *believe it, you can make* her *believe it.*

He did everything he could to match Katie's charm. With a combined look of sincerity and desperation he said, "It's just that I need to visit my grandmother before she dies. She's in Junin and if I don't get there today, the doctor says it will be too late." He managed to force a single tear, which dripped slowly out of his eye and down his cheek.

The woman behind the counter watched, and something about her changed. Her previous look, stoic and businesslike, softened. Tears welled in her eyes. She was touched by his story. She looked over the counter both left and right then leaned forward. "I know of someone nearby," she whispered. "He could rent you a motorbike. Can you ride a motorcycle?"

"I would do anything to see her," Luke replied.

The woman jotted down a name and an address and handed it to Luke. "Go outside, turn right and go three blocks then turn left and go one block. You will see a sign for the Garaje de Automóviles. Ask for my cousin Guillermo. I will call and let him know you are coming."

Luke took the piece of paper and thanked her profusely.

The four blocks to Garaje de Automóviles went by in a flash. He was nervous about meeting Guillermo and about riding a motorcycle in a strange city. He wasn't sure what to expect. When he got there, his concerns were put to rest. The "motorcycle" wasn't really a motorcycle at all. It was a glorified moped, and Guillermo cared more about the cash in Luke's pocket than his age or his riding ability.

* * *

The sun was just peaking over the horizon when Luke drove out of the city limits. He merged onto the highway and headed into the hills. According to Guillermo, the motorcycle had a top speed of fifty miles per hour. Luke pushed it to the limits. He opened up the throttle and bent his body forward, willing the machine faster. After an hour of driving, he pulled off the highway and onto a dirt road leading up the mountain. The next thirty minutes severely tested his strength and driving skills. The road turned at sharp angles; the season's rains had washed away large areas of dirt, leaving a rugged and uneven path. By the time the old weathered church and its graveyard came into sight, his muscles were tired, his bottom was sore, and his body was ready to collapse.

Luke hid the bike behind the church and raced through the cemetery. It had been almost a year since he had been here with Aunt Janine and her crew but he still remembered the path that would lead him to the secret entrance and contemplated how he would open the passage by himself. Much to his surprise, the entryway was already open. He pulled his trusty lantern from his backpack, got down on his knees, and entered the hole.

Luke had an odd feeling. Sure he had been here before, but something about this scenario was strangely familiar. The musty smell, the moist clay like dirt that clung to his jeans, the aging support beams, all triggered some deep hidden memory. He could feel the tunnel closing in on him. Not usually prone to claustrophobia, he had to remind himself to breathe. Despite the anxiety that was growing inside of him, he pushed forward.

At spots, the ceiling of this old tunnel had collapsed and been re-dug. He squirmed through on his belly, holding his breath as the dirt crumbled from above. God knows what was falling in his hair and down the back of his shirt; a spider web clung to his face, an eerie chill shot up the back of his neck. He hoped upon hope that there was no hairy spider to go along with that web. He hoped upon hope that the fragile rotting frame would not collapse and drop tons of smothering dirt on top of him. These thoughts, these fears consumed his overworked mind. At least he had his lantern, a single beam of light guiding the way through the unknown.

When the tunnel opened to an underground room constructed entirely from stone, he exhaled a deep sigh of relief. The single beam of light from his lantern lit small sections at a time. It was just as he remembered. There were intricate designs on the floor, as well as around and above the doorways--four in all--plus the tunnel that brought him there. The room was circular, the ceiling a dome--all of it expertly crafted. Luke knelt down in the center of the room and wiped away the dust on the floor. With each pass of his hand, the details of the compass came into view. He gripped the dial at the center and turned, first to the north, then to the east, then to the south and then to the west. Each turn of the dial caused a stone door to shift and open. When the last door popped from its locked position, Luke ran over and pushed the heavy stone out of the way. A long steady hiss escaped from the tunnel behind.

That eerie feeling grew stronger. He shined the lantern into the corridor and followed the beam of light. There were passageways leading off the main path, both to the left and to the right. At each offshoot he stopped, inspected the gateway, and moved on. He knew these would not lead him to his destination. He continued until he reached the end of the tunnel where there were three doors, one in front, one to the left, and one to the right. Each door had a dial on it, similar to the one he found on the floor of the circular room. Luke faced the door to the left and turned the dial right. He faced the opposite door and turned the dial left. He then approached the dial on the last door, the door in the center, and turned it up towards the ceiling. A strange clicking sound echoed throughout the corridor, and the floor began to shake. His feet slipped. Desperately, he grabbed for the walls, but there was nothing to hold on to. His fingers grasped, but it was useless, he could not stop the downward slide. His stomach jumped into his throat, worse than the Wicked Wiley roller coaster at Pirate Land. It made him nauseous, and he lost his grip on the lamp.

Helplessly, he fell into the pitch black abyss. The sudden drop was terrifying. His body slammed against a solid wall. Without warning, the shaft changed direction, bending from vertical to horizontal. The unexpected turn contorted and twisted his body. By the time he was expelled from the shaft, he was spinning uncontrollably. Finally, he slowed to a stop, dazed and confused, on a hard stone floor deep inside the earth.

The sudden jolt to his system made recovery difficult; his head was dizzy, his body battered. He needed to regain his composure and prepare for whatever might come next, but it was dark and his brain wouldn't cooperate. The sound of small feet scurrying in the darkness sent a shiver up his spine. He dragged his unwilling body across the cold stone floor, searching with his hands in the dark, unable to stand. Fortunately, he found his lantern. It was at the base of the shaft. It seemed to be in one piece. He banged it against his thigh and was rewarded with the sweet relief of light.

He scanned the area; the beam of light guided his view. This room was unlike the first chamber; this floor was laid with stone tiles, these walls were squared, and this ceiling flat. One of the walls was covered with beautiful, intricate stained glass designs. Luke moved the light around the room. He saw sconces on the walls, and ornate chairs fit for a king. He remembered the last time he had been in this chamber, trapped with his family and left to die.

But then, a horrifying sight, there, slumped over a table in the center of the room, was a man. From behind, Luke saw the familiar faded leather jacket and blue baseball cap that could only mean one thing. On this table, in this underground chamber deep below the surface of the earth, was the lifeless form of his hero, Uncle Al. Luke felt for a pulse, but there was none. He tried to shake him, but it was no use; he gave no response no matter how hard he tried.

This couldn't be happening. It had to be a dream, a nightmare. Surely he would wake up and all this would be over. He fought back the tears. The pain welled up within him. He closed his eyes, but it didn't help. Uncle Al was dead.

A voice from above startled him. "Luke! Luke, are you down there?"

Luke turned around to see a large form whip into the room and come to a screeching halt at his feet. He directed his lantern down and was greeted by Mom and her stunned face. He dropped the lantern and grabbed her in a tight hug, unable to hold back his tears any longer.

40. Too Much to Handle

Together, Luke and Mom managed to get Uncle Al's body back up the slide, through the tunnels, and to the graveyard. They agreed that Uncle Al would have wanted to be buried at one of Soren Jacobsen's sites, and so they dug a grave and laid the man to rest near the site where the clock had first been discovered.

They said a few prayers and then covered him with dirt. Luke was still finishing his final prayer when Mom headed back towards the tunnel.

"Where are you going?"

"Back inside the tomb," Mom replied.

"Are you joking?" Luke responded incredulously.

Mom came back to him. "We've come all this way to find the last piece of the puzzle. It's right in there."

Luke couldn't have been more confused. They had just buried his Uncle, his hero, and all Mom could think about was another clue.

"I know what you're thinking," Mom said. She tried to bring Luke into a hug.

He pulled away. "You don't know what I'm thinking, and you don't know how I feel. He just died and you're still going forward with this?"

"Luke…," Mom said, fighting back tears, "we travelled thousands of miles to solve a mystery and the answer is right in there."

Luke didn't know what to say. He was hurt in so many ways he couldn't describe it.

"It's what Uncle Al would have wanted," Mom rationalized.

Luke thought on the words. *Is this really what Uncle Al would have wanted?* In a stupor, he followed Mom into the tunnel, unable to think, unable to put cognitive thoughts together. They crawled through the tunnel, passed through the domed room, and slid down the slide to their destination. No words were spoken between them.

When they shined the lantern on the walls, they saw the stained glass windows and marveled at their beauty. They scanned the remainder of the room, and at the base of the wall, inside the slide that brought them there, they found what they were looking for: an image of a boy swinging a sword. Not just any sword, Curtana. And not just any boy, it was Luke with his sandy blonde hair, glasses, and a look on his face that showed fear, uncertainty and determination all at once. A triangle wrapped in a serpentine vine surrounded Luke and his swinging sword crushed three flags, one black, one white and one green. The picture made it clear. Luke knew where this grand mystery was leading him. He knew what Soren Jacobsen intended for him to do, even if he didn't know why. In that moment he felt just like the boy in the image, filled with apprehension, but determined to fulfill his destiny.

Mom gripped his hand and together they took in the deeper meaning of Soren's secrets: some things are bigger than any one person, bigger than life, and bigger than death. This is what Uncle Al would have wanted.

You Too Can Join the Journey

The Stolen Adventure Fan Club

Includes quarterly e-Newsletters featuring:

- **Previews of upcoming books**
- **Additional Stories not found anywhere else**
- **Behind The Scenes Secrets**
- **Images of Your Favorite Characters**
- **And more…**

Visit the web site to join
www.stolenadventure.com

Check out all the books in The Stolen Adventure Series:

- The Stolen Adventure
- The Quest for Curtana
- The Journey to Joyeuse
- The Search for Soren's Secrets

www.ingramcontent.com/pod-product-compliance
Lightning Source LLC
Chambersburg PA
CBHW070613130626
46556CB00001B/356